MURDER BY PLUM PUDDING

A 1920S COZY HISTORICAL MYSTERY

A GINGER GOLD MYSTERY
BOOK 11

LEE STRAUSS

Previously published as part of the boxed set titled Six Merry Little Murders.

Library and Archives Canada Cataloguing in Publication Title: Murder by plum pudding : a cozy historical 1920s mystery / Lee Strauss. Names: Strauss, Lee (Novelist), author. Series: Strauss, Lee (Novelist). Ginger Gold mystery ; 11. Description: Series statement: A Ginger Gold mystery ; 11 Identifiers: Canadiana (print) 20190193697 | Canadiana (ebook) 20190193700 | ISBN 9781774090671 (softcover) | ISBN 9781774090664 (hardcover) | ISBN 9781774090688 (IngramSpark softcover) | ISBN 9781988677996 (Kindle) | ISBN 9781774090657 (EPUB) | ISBN: 978-1-77409-331-3 (bookvault) ISBN 978-1-77409-388-7 (d2d) Classification: LCC PS8637.T739 M375 2019 | DDC C813/.6—dc23

GINGER GOLD MYSTERIES

(IN ORDER)

1

The journal remained tucked away in the bottom drawer of Mrs. Ginger Reed's bedside table, along with a photo of her first husband, Daniel, Lord Gold.

From under carefully folded silk scarves Ginger lifted out the items, then sat on the edge of the large four-poster bed she shared with her new husband, Chief Inspector Basil Reed. And Boss. Her pet had jumped up and stretched out at the foot of the bed. He panted a doggy smile, then closed his large brown eyes and promptly started snoring. Ginger chuckled. "Oh, Bossy. Life is so easy for you."

She stared at the sepia and white image of the handsome soldier. Though she loved Basil with all of her heart, Daniel had been her first. His death, one of thousands during the Great War, had shattered her. The loss was tremendous, and the burden of guilt she felt was at times suffocating.

Oh, the war! The shadows it cast were long-reaching, even seven years after it had ended. Ginger's time in the British Secret Service would remain such—secret—and she alone would bear the weight of knowing she could have saved her husband and didn't.

She set the photograph aside and opened the well-worn leather journal, flipping through its pages, and perhaps because it was the day before Christmas Eve, she stopped on the date of December 24th, 1912, the year before she and Daniel had wed. Her familiar though youthful script began:

It's a tradition for the Hartigan family to volunteer at Christ Church on Salem Street to help serve Christmas dinner to the poor and underprivileged citizens of Boston—a charitable effort driven by the determination and insistence of my warm-hearted father, and resisted equally by my headstrong stepmother, Sally.

Ginger chuckled, but she felt a twinge in her heart.

It'd been a while now since she'd laid eyes on her flamboyant stepmother, Sally Hartigan, and her capricious half-sister, Louisa. Louisa, so full of life and energy, was easy to miss, but the sentimentality of the season had softened Ginger's heart enough to find room there for her difficult stepmother as well.

"The church is doing a good enough job without my having to get my gloves dirty," Sally said as we sat around the warmth of the fire in the sitting room. *"Can't we just enjoy a quiet and carefree Christmas Eve for once, George?"*

"We are blessed beyond measure," Father said, like he does every year. *"Christmas is about giving, and as members of the elite, it's doubly important that one doesn't forget those whose lives are a daily struggle."*

Sally wasn't about to go down without a fight. *"Think about Louisa."*

Louisa, who was playing quietly with a porcelain doll, glanced up at the mention of her name.

Sally continued, *"Would you have your own young daughter exposed to who knows what ailment? Last year a man stood right behind her and coughed."*

I noticed that Sally specified father's younger daughter, even though I was also in the room. Clearly, she wasn't worried that a stranger might inadvertently spew spittle in my direction.

"I do think about Louisa, which is precisely why I insist on going."

"I'm not sure we're doing those people much good. They'll just learn to depend on handouts."

"It's Christmas," I said, siding with Father.

Sally's nose jutted higher. "They're immigrants."

I was aghast. "We're immigrants!"

Louisa smirked. "I'm not."

Father was not swayed, and at five o'clock in the evening, the four of us bundled up in our fur-trimmed winter coats, muffs, and hats, and rode in our enclosed carriage as our driver directed the horses to the church hall.

Ginger was interrupted by her young maid Lizzie, dressed in a black frock covered by a white apron, and on her head, covering a short-fringed haircut, a white servant's cap. She curtsied slightly before speaking.

"You've got visitors, madam."

"I have?" Ginger marked the journal entry with a piece of string before closing the book and setting it aside. "But who? I'm not expecting anyone until tomorrow."

Mr. Doyle of New York and his wife were due to arrive then. He was a former associate and friend of her late father's, though Ginger had never met the

Doyles herself. He'd written several weeks ago asking if they could stay. Apparently, the man had a business idea he thought she'd be interested in. She couldn't imagine what that might be, but she hadn't had the heart to say no.

Lizzie's pixie-thin face grew rosy. "They asked me not to say, madam. They want to keep it a surprise."

Ginger raised a thinly plucked brow. She didn't like surprises and her family and staff knew this about her.

Lizzie added quickly, "It's two ladies, madam."

Ginger didn't want to torture the girl's conscience. With Boss at her heels, she strolled down the corridor past the bedrooms to the landing above an ornate staircase that curved down to the black and white marble entrance below. A grand chandelier hung high above the entrance, its electric lights illuminating the entrance hall. Tall windows flanked either side of a thick wooden door, and standing in front of it were the very two ladies Ginger had just been thinking of.

Louisa shouted, "Surprise!" She held out her arms, clad in burgundy velvet. The shin-length coat had ornamental stitching, and the collar, cuffs, and entire length of the edging were trimmed with thick grey fur. Ginger recognised the quality of the *tailleur de luxe* item at once.

"Louisa? Sally?" Their names escaped Ginger's lips as she hurried down the stairs. "I'm astonished!" She accepted Louisa's warm embrace, and a shorter, tenser version of a hug from her stepmother.

Ginger reined in her flustered feelings and adopted a welcoming smile. "Why didn't you tell me you were coming?"

"It wouldn't have been a surprise, then, silly," Louisa said. "I had to make Mama promise she wouldn't send a telegram."

Sally Hartigan was an attractive brunette with early signs of greying. She had fine lines around green, cat-like eyes, which deepened as she smirked, and Ginger could tell her stepmother rather enjoyed Ginger's discomfiture. Though they had never been outright enemies, their mutual longing for George Hartigan's full attention had made them more like competitors than family. Her father's passing hadn't changed that.

Pippins, Ginger's devoted septuagenarian butler, having heard the commotion was soon at her side.

"Pippins, you remember my sister, Louisa?" Louisa had spent a number of weeks as Ginger's guest the summer before. "And this is her mother, Mrs. Hartigan."

Sally had never been one to consider staff as anything more than a useful appliance such as an electric mixer or vacuum cleaner, and she'd rather kiss a frog, Ginger thought, than look a butler or maid in the eye. Her stepmother kept her gaze averted.

Pippins, unruffled by her slight, bowed his tall, slender form, his aged shoulders hunched slightly. His cornflower-blue eyes twinkled. "May I take your coats?"

"Louisa wasn't kidding when she said you lived in a mansion," Sally said. Her lips pulled up in an approving smile but her eyes remained indifferent. Like most Londoners fighting against the grey and gloom of a damp winter, Ginger had decorated the place with an abundance of green. Holly and ivy twined along the wooden railing and banister and wreathed over the door frames.

"It's hardly a mansion," Ginger said.

"It's twice the size of our brownstone in Boston."

Ginger heard the hint of envy. She and Louisa shared the same father, and when George Hartigan had died, he'd left the brownstone to Louisa, to be shared with her mother, and his London home to

Ginger. And rightly so, Ginger thought, since she'd been born in London and lived in Hartigan House until she was eight years old, a bleak time in her young life, when her father had carted her off to America so he could marry Sally.

To Sally she said, "Surely you've been here before?"

Sally wiggled well-bejewelled fingers. "It was such a long time ago."

"Pippins, please inform the kitchen that we have guests and will take tea in the sitting room."

"Are you going to leave our luggage to sit in the rain?" Sally asked.

"Your luggage?"

"Yes, the taxi driver left it on the stoop," Louisa said. "You don't mind if we stay with you, do you? I know you have tons of room."

Ginger held in her dismay. It was Christmas, and she could hardly turn them out into the streets. "Of course not." To Pippins she added, "Please ask Lizzie and Grace to prepare rooms, and ask Clement to take our guests' luggage upstairs."

Pippins disappeared down the corridor towards the back of the house, whilst Ginger led her guests through the double doors of the sitting room, decorated in a modern style with rose and saffron straight-lined furniture angled towards a stone fireplace, a jade Persian carpet, wooden coffee tables, and a sideboard equipped with drinks and glasses. Tall windows added light.

Sally, with her twisted sense of intuition, gravitated to Ginger's favourite chair and lowered herself with an exaggerated exhalation. "It's a relief to spend part of the winter out of Boston, but it's not as pleasant here as Louisa promised."

Louisa came to her own defence. "It was summer when I was here last. Besides, it might be dreary and grey, but at least there's no snow."

Tea was delivered and Ginger poured for Louisa and Sally. "Milk and sugar?" she asked. Ginger waited for the nods she expected, added the extras and delivered the tea on their matching floral saucers.

Sally stared at the Waterhouse painting of *The Mermaid* over the mantel. "Some things never change."

Ginger had done a lot of redecorating on her return to London, but she had kept the classic art piece above the hearth. The mermaid, innocently naked to her waist, had long red hair that tumbled over her shoulders and delicately preserved her modesty. The mythical creature reminded Ginger of her mother, not only with the colour of her hair, but the sparkle in her eyes.

"It's rather vulgar, don't you think?" Sally continued.

"I like it," Louisa said. "It's bold, and symbolises modern feminism. We women have more freedoms than ever before, but not nearly enough, in my estimation."

Ginger couldn't help but smile at her sister.

Louisa seemed unaware of Ginger's amusement and demanded, "Where is Felicia? You haven't sent her back to the country, have you? *Have you?* And her cranky grandmother too? *That* wouldn't be so tragic."

"Louisa!" Ginger scolded. "Felicia is doing some last-minute Christmas shopping and Ambrosia is resting. They will join us for an early dinner."

"And your husband," Louisa said. "You're still married?"

"Of course I'm still married." Ginger snorted lightly. "He's out with Scout, getting a tree."

"I'm still upset that I wasn't at your wedding," Louisa said. She scowled at Sally when she said this. Louisa had only just returned to Boston after a rebellious trip to London, and Sally hadn't been about to let her daughter out of her sight so quickly afterwards.

"Louisa says you've adopted a grown street boy?" Sally asked. Her disapproval was hardly concealed behind her pretend shock.

"Yes. It's providence, you could say," Ginger said.

Sally lifted her teacup to her lips, hiding, as it were, behind it. "I suppose a person might do anything to have a child they can call their own."

"Scout is a very special boy, and my son now, Sally. I expect you, as my guest, to show him the same respect that you show me."

Belatedly, Ginger realised she wasn't asking much of her stepmother.

Sally's lips twitched in a half smile. "Certainly, Ginger. I'm only intrigued with how your life has turned out. George would be—"

"Pleased," Ginger said, finishing for her. "Father would be very pleased. In fact, you'll be happy to hear that I'm continuing one of his favourite traditions—feeding the poor at a local church."

The sounds of men's voices and a child's laughter from the other side of the doors reached them and Ginger jumped to her feet.

"Basil and Scout are back."

Louisa was quick to follow Ginger into the hall, whilst Sally moved more slowly, looking as if she was barely hanging on to a sliver of patience.

"Where do you want it, love?" Basil asked, when he saw her. His face was flushed with the exertion, only emphasising his handsome features. Dark hair was oiled back and to one side and trimmed around shapely ears, where it showed a hint of grey. His hazel eyes, wrinkling at the corners, sparkled as he gazed at Ginger with admiration. Married only a few months, it was easy for Ginger and Basil to forget that they weren't alone. She smiled back with appreciation.

"Basil!" Louisa squealed.

The shock that overtook Basil's face was enough to make Ginger break out in laughter.

"Louisa and Sally have surprised us, love," she explained. "They're here for Christmas."

Basil removed his hat and gloves and extended a hand to Sally. "It's a pleasure to meet you, Mrs. Hartigan," he said.

Sally's countenance brightened remarkably. Basil had that effect on the gentler sex. "Likewise. Louisa, you weren't exaggerating when you said the chief inspector was handsome."

Unsatisfied with a mere handshake, Louisa

threw herself into Basil's arms. "We're sister and brother now!"

Basil chuckled, cast a questioning glance over Louisa's shoulder at Ginger, and said, "Indeed." He peeled his new sibling off, and used the action to remove his jacket.

"I'll take that for you, sir," Pippins said.

"Thank you, Pippins," Basil returned.

Scout had managed to hide himself behind Ginger during the exchange. Ginger took his hand and gently pulled him into view. "This is Scout. Scout, this is Mrs. Hartigan and you remember my sister, Louisa."

"That makes me an aunt, does it not?" Louisa said, more to herself than to Scout, as if the concept had occurred to her for the first time.

"Yes," Ginger said. "This is Aunt Louisa."

Scout bowed respectfully.

Louisa held her hand out and Scout shook it. "All kinds of new family today," she said. "First a brother and now a nephew."

Sally remained quiet, her chin turned upwards.

"The tree?" Basil said.

"Oh yes, the drawing room, please," Ginger said. The drawing room lay opposite the sitting room on the other side of the main doors along the entrance way. Basil and Scout wrestled the tree through the French doors in a manner that made Ginger bite her lip to keep from smiling too widely with the joy she felt at the sight.

Ginger presented the drawing room to the Hartigan ladies. Art deco wallpaper, in hues of ivory, grey, and green, made the large room feel chic. A baby grand piano stood impressively in one corner while a brick fireplace took the opposite wall. A green velvet settee and matching pincushion chairs trimmed ornately with polished wood stood around a large coffee table in the centre. On the walls were two portraits, one each of Ginger's parents. Her mother, as the wife before Sally, was of apparent keen interest to Ginger's stepmother, and the woman spent a noticeable amount of time staring at the image.

"She had red hair, didn't she?" Sally said. "So unbecoming."

Ginger's hand automatically went to her own red bob. Being redheaded wasn't considered an asset as far as fashion and beauty went, but Ginger hadn't done poorly by it. She'd embraced what the good Lord had given her, and in fact, loved how it set her apart from most.

"Father found ginger hair to be a lovely thing,

obviously," Ginger said. "They were very much in love."

That last bit was an unnecessary jab, and Ginger immediately regretted it. Sally Hartigan had been married to her father for longer than Ginger's mother had. Her stepmother had a way of bringing out the worst in her.

2

Christmas Eve morning was a relaxed affair, with everyone helping themselves to the breakfast buffet Mrs. Beasley had masterfully provided whenever they sauntered down to the morning room. Ginger and Scout along with Ambrosia were the early risers, joined later by Basil and Felicia. Ginger drank another cup of tea as an excuse to prolong her stay whilst Scout ran off with Boss, and Ambrosia sought out her maid, Langley, in order to give her further instructions regarding her needs for the day. Sally and Louisa were apparently enjoying a nice lie-in, suffering as they probably were from their long journey.

"Did you sleep well, love?" Ginger asked Basil.

"Splendidly. Murder rarely takes place over Christmas, which is jolly good for my department."

The goodness of mankind could be seen once in a while, and Ginger was reminded of the Christmas of 1914, when British and German soldiers called a one-day truce, and instead of shooting at one another played a game of football and exchanged gifts.

"I slept marvellously too," Felicia quipped as she shook open a linen napkin and placed it on her lap. "Thanks for asking."

"You've never had a problem with sleeping, dear, since I've known you," Ginger replied with a chuckle. "Which is why it never occurs to me to enquire."

Basil and Felicia had almost finished their plates of scrambled eggs, grilled kippers, fried sliced tomatoes, and buttered toast, when Sally and Louisa strolled in.

"Now I remember why I never came back before now," Sally said. "Such long stretches away from home wreak havoc with a person's beauty sleep."

Ginger got to her feet and poured a cup of coffee for her stepmother, adding milk and sugar the way she knew Sally liked it, and handed it to her.

"God bless you," Sally said. She blew on the

brew carefully before taking a sip. "Not bad. It hits the spot."

Ginger watched as her American relatives skipped over the black pudding and baked beans and stuck to the scrambled eggs, bacon, and toast.

"We have quite a large gathering for dinner tomorrow," Ginger said.

"Any handsome, single gentlemen?" Louisa said. "Hopefully with money?"

"There are plenty of suitable bachelors in America, Louisa," Sally said. Ginger didn't blame Sally for wanting to keep her only child close to her on American soil.

"Speaking of Americans," Ginger said. "Do you happen to know a Mr. and Mrs. Doyle from New York?"

Sally turned her cat eyes on Ginger. "I believe I do. Why?"

"They're coming for Christmas."

"Is that so?"

Ginger was impressed with Sally's calmness about the arrival of more guests. She wasn't one who liked to share the stage, but then she had come unannounced. "Yes, they're staying for a couple of days," Ginger answered.

"I see," Sally murmured.

"How well do you know the Doyles?" Ginger asked. Mr. Doyle had made it sound like he and Ginger's father had been good friends.

"Not well at all. He had dealings with your father, but we only met socially once or twice. Years ago, really." Sally sipped her coffee then deftly changed the subject. "Who else is coming?"

"Basil's parents, Mr. and Mrs. Reed," Ginger began. Basil's gaze flickered her way with a look of helpless apology. His parents hadn't made life particularly easy for Ginger. She continued, "Our good friend Dr. Gupta and his wife, and Mr. and Mrs. Davenport, Reed family friends."

Louisa pouted. "Not a single gentleman in the mix."

"This is England, and unfortunately, quite normal since the war," Felicia said. "The female to male ratio is dreadfully skewed. Far more of the former than the latter."

This revelation caused a frown of consternation to come over Louisa. Still so young and naïve, Ginger thought. Checking her wristwatch, Ginger was astonished at how fast the morning had gone.

"It's almost time to go."

"Go where?" Felicia asked.

"It's a Christmas Eve tradition in the Hartigan

family to help serve Christmas dinner for the less fortunate. Reverend Hill is expecting us at St. George's Church."

Sally stood. "Not for this Hartigan, I'm afraid."

"Nor this one," Louisa said. She stared at Basil pointedly. "Did you know that Ginger once gave her winter coat away? Silly girl. And on such a cold Christmas Eve."

Before Ginger could respond to the accusation, Sally cut in. "I'll be spending the remainder of my morning resting in my room. I'm sure you understand."

"Of course," Ginger said. Truthfully, she was glad to leave Sally and Louisa behind. They made behaving in a Christ-like manner rather difficult.

GINGER QUICKLY GOT ready to go, looking in on Scout's bedroom before heading downstairs. The letter to Father Christmas she'd helped him compose was sitting on his desk, and a clean grey sock hung on the bedpost waiting for the jolly man's visit, but Scout was nowhere to be seen. Despite his change in status, Ginger's adopted son preferred to play outside with Boss and help Clement take care of the horses.

"Are we all going to fit in my motorcar?" Ginger asked when she approached Felicia and Basil who stood waiting. Felicia wore a green velvet day dress with gold embroidery on the shoulders and the bell sleeves and skirt in a contrasting magenta. She was obviously not concerned about standing out.

"It's just the three of us," Felicia said. "Grandmama says she needs the rest if she's going to face 'the hordes' coming for Christmas tomorrow."

"It's hardly a horde," Ginger said, though it was a good thing the dining room table had plenty of leaves. "Going back to today, Scout's not joining us, at least not this year."

Felicia hummed. "Yes, I suppose it would be in bad form to parade his good fortune to his own lot, and at Christmastime, no less."

Basil jingled a set of keys. "How about we take the Austin?" Basil's winter-green 1922 Austin 7 wasn't as luxurious as Ginger's new ivory and chrome Crossley, but perhaps it was better suited for the task at hand. Ginger wouldn't have to put up with Felicia's complaints about her driving if Basil took the wheel. She smiled in agreement. "That would be lovely, darling."

Taking the door leading to the back garden where the garage and stables were located, Ginger paused for a moment to peek into the kitchen. Mrs. Beasley and her staff were bustling about. Short and stout with a round pink face and a serious countenance, Mrs. Beasley was an excellent cook and house manager.

"How are you, Mrs. Beasley?" Ginger said.

Like a fluttering butterfly who suddenly stilled, Mrs. Beasley gawked at Ginger. "I'm fine, madam, and everything is prepared. The duck for tonight and the goose for tomorrow. There are plenty of cakes and puddings. The plum pudding has been ready for several weeks now. Just the brandy butter to prepare."

Ginger smiled warmly at the verbose woman, feeling quite grateful for her good and loyal staff. She'd heard horror stories from others who weren't so fortunate with their servants and Ginger intended to reward all hers generously come Boxing Day. "Do take a moment to rest and enjoy a cup of tea today," she said.

"I will, madam," Mrs. Beasley returned. "Thank you."

Outside, the sky was murky grey and the air damp but not terribly cold. Nothing that a little body heat wouldn't take care of with the three of them in the Austin—Basil and Ginger in the front seat and Felicia in the back. As they drove along the south side of Kensington Gardens in the direction of the City of London, Ginger couldn't help but think about how different this ride was to the one she'd written about in her journal. Such a far cry from the crushing cold of the windy Boston Nor'easters and the wooden horse-drawn carriages driven by brave coachmen

St. George's Church, an eighteenth-century limestone structure which extended back from the street, had a square tower at the front. A cemetery sat on one side while the attached hall extended on the other, all of which were made glossy and darker with the rain.

Ginger and the good Reverend Oliver Hill had struck up a close friendship over their shared ambitions of helping the poor. Together they had started the Child Wellness Project, which was now sponsoring the second annual Christmas Eve dinner.

"This won't take all afternoon will it?" Felicia asked.

"Oh mercy," Ginger said. "You're sounding like Sally and Louisa just now."

"I'm not," Felicia insisted. "About those two, did you really not know they were coming?"

Ginger shook her head. "They wanted to surprise me, and they did!"

"Wouldn't they have been surprised if we'd gone elsewhere for Christmas? Some people go south in the winter."

Inside the hall, tables were set up in long rows and volunteers had done their best to decorate with boughs of green, candles, and even a tree in the corner. A grandmotherly parishioner played Christmas carols on a piano. The air smelled of roast goose and potatoes. Ginger was pleased to see needy families together in attendance along with many of the street urchins that came to the weekly dinners.

"I'm sure Mrs. Davis could use help in the kitchen," Ginger said. "Felicia, I'll meet you there in a moment. I'm going to speak to Oliver and Matilda first."

Oliver spotted Ginger and Basil and approached with long strides. His hair, as red as Ginger's, was oiled back, his face freckled, and his smile wide. "Happy Christmas!" he proclaimed loudly. He shook Basil's hand, "Happy Christmas, Chief Inspector!"

Ginger and Basil each returned, "Happy Christmas."

"How is Matilda?" Ginger asked.

"Very well, thank you. She's helping Mrs. Davis. We're nearly ready to begin." He waved a long arm. "Isn't this jolly?"

Ginger couldn't help but share in his joy and laughed. "It is!"

They were approached by a pleasant-looking man in his thirties. His eyes were particularly noteworthy, as he had a noticeable case of heterochromia, with one hazel eye and one blue. His smooth skin crinkled as he smiled. "Can I assume these are our sponsors?"

"Oh yes," Oliver replied. "Please allow me to make introductions. This is Mr. Alan Lester, a new member of our church. Lester, this is Chief Inspector and Mrs. Reed."

Ginger offered a gloved hand. "It's good to meet you, Mr. Lester," she said. "How kind of you to volunteer."

"I'm alone and single," he said, not at all remorsefully. "These people are like family to me now."

"How wonderful!"

Basil and Oliver had moved along, engaged in light conversation, leaving Ginger with Mr. Lester.

"I understand you've quite recently returned to London from America?" he said.

"Yes. From Boston."

"Reverend Hill told me you're the former Lady Gold. My sister tells me she is going to be staying with you."

"Your sister? Oh, you must mean Mrs. Doyle!"

"Yes, that's right. She wrote to tell me they were coming, and unfortunately I have no room for them to stay with me."

"Well, you must join us for Christmas dinner then, unless you have other plans?"

"I don't, as a matter of fact, and I'd be pleased to join you. I don't see my sister very often and every minute more is a blessing."

"Very good." Ginger removed her coat as she was feeling quite warmed up. She smiled to herself. Wouldn't Louisa and Felicia be surprised now! "I'm needed in the kitchen, Mr. Lester, but we'll speak tomorrow if we don't have a chance to do so again today."

Mr. Lester nodded as she turned to the coat rack in the kitchen and deposited her things. "Sorry, I got caught up in conversation," she said to everyone there. "How can I help?"

3

*I*t was the first Christmas Eve for Ginger with a child of her own. Even though Scout, in his knickerbockers and flat cap, was, nearing the age of twelve, hardly a young child, he was small for his age with the wide-eyed innocence of a lad much younger. For the first time, he was seeing the extravagant side of life for himself.

Christmas music played on the gramophone as they decorated the tree with tinsel, colourful ornaments, and small candles. Once they had finished, they enjoyed Mrs. Beasley's bite-sized mince pies and a glass of sloe gin.

Sally and Louisa sat on either end of the velvet settee, while Ginger lounged in a matching rose and jade pincushion chair. She crossed her rayon-covered legs and smoothed out the satin finish of her gown. Facing the roaring fire, Ginger was soothed by the glowing embers. She loved Christmas, with the scent of the tree, the flickering lights of the candles, and the snapping of the yule log. The sloe gin tickled her tongue and Ginger felt a sense of overall well-being.

Basil sat in the matching chair perpendicular to hers. "Shall I start reading *A Christmas Carol*?"

"Now?" Sally asked.

"It's a tradition," Basil said, "for someone to tell a favourite Christmas story on Christmas Eve.

"Not the one with Jesus at the centre?" Louisa quipped.

Basil grinned. "That one will be covered at length at church tomorrow morning."

"Scout, go and get the letter you wrote to Father Christmas," Ginger instructed. "We need to burn it in the fireplace so the smoke can relay our wishes."

Scout gave Ginger a sideways glance. His time as a hungry waif had taught him that Father Christmas was quite prejudiced when it came to children getting wishes granted on Christmas morning, but he shrugged and headed upstairs, apparently willing to play along.

Ginger felt a wave of sadness, knowing that she had missed the stage with her newly adopted son where make-believe was whimsical. Still, she felt she could sneak in one more childish game.

"Surely, you're not leaving Santa Claus out of the picture, are you?" Louisa said. "And a bottle of Coca Cola? Besides, mailing letters to the North Pole makes a whole lot more sense than burning them in the fire."

Ginger glared at Louisa, who simply sipped her glass of sloe gin, then smiled back smugly.

Scout returned with his letter, and Ginger made a show of producing one as well. Ginger who thought that Scout might like a train set or model aeroplane, had planted the idea in his mind, and helped him compose his wishes, so that when his gifts were opened in the morning and he found his request there, he couldn't help but be astonished.

"I added a wish, Mum," he said. "I hope that's all right."

Ginger eyed Scout with interest. He wasn't the type to be greedy. "What's your extra wish?" She had to ask in order to make it come true.

"My wish is that Marvin would have a good Christmas and that we'll see each other again soon."

Ginger's heart squeezed with emotion. Poor Scout!

"Who's Marvin?" Louisa asked.

"Marvin is Scout's older cousin," Ginger said. "He's in the navy now, and couldn't be back for Christmas."

Thankfully, the spotlight was removed from Scout with the arrival of Ambrosia and Felicia.

"It's very warm in here," Ambrosia said. Still bound to her practice of wearing a corset, she sat overly upright in a wing-backed chair and rested slightly against the silver end of her walking stick. "Is it necessary for it to be so hot? This isn't India."

"The fire has receded," Ginger said. "It'll cool down before you know it."

"I like it," Felicia said. "I'm so tired of cold and gloomy."

"Felicia, darling," Ginger began, "Would you play the piano for us? Be a brick and lead us in some Christmas carols and then Basil's going to read to us."

Felicia sauntered to the shiny black grand piano, opened the lid and began to play a joyous medley of "We Three Kings", "Hark the Herald Angels Sing", and "Silent Night". Even Ambrosia seemed to forget herself and joined in.

When they'd exhausted Felicia's Christmas music repertoire, Basil produced a volume of Charles Dickens' *A Christmas Carol*, and regaled them all with the tale of the three Christmas Ghosts. For once, Scout appeared dumbfounded.

"Have you not heard this story before?" Ginger asked.

"No, Mum. It's a first for me. Jolly good story, it is. I feel like I know Tiny Tim, hisself."

Basil closed the volume, marking his place. "I'll finish it tomorrow night."

Scout barely had a chance to protest when the doorbell chimed. Pippins answered the door.

"Merry Christmas, my good fellow!" The loud male voice reached them in the drawing room, and was most definitely American. "I do believe Mrs. Gold is expecting us. I'm Mr. Arnold Doyle."

4

*G*inger awoke to the church clocks striking the hour on Christmas morning. She counted eight and, with Boss nudging her cheek with his wet nose, decided it was a good time to rise. Not wanting to wake Basil, Ginger quietly dressed, choosing a Madeleine Vionnet of baby-blue silk crepe de Chine with a low white satin sash ending in a large bow at the hips. She added a pearl choker necklace and matching pearl earrings, and finished with a light touch of makeup.

"You look beautiful."

Ginger turned to Basil's raspy morning voice.

"Sorry, love," she said. "I didn't mean to wake you."

Basil raised himself onto his elbows, and Ginger

bit her lip at his tousled hair and pyjama shirt buttoned askew.

"I'm just grateful that you're able to get the time off work." Ginger kissed her husband, then went in search of her son. She expected to find him opening the small gifts inside his stocking, but found him sleeping soundly in his bed.

"Hey, sleepyhead," she said. "It's Christmas!"

Scout snapped awake and threw his blankets off. "Oh, Mum, I didn't miss it, did I?"

"Not at all. Clean up and get dressed and meet me for breakfast."

The morning room, which had tall French windows overlooking the back garden, was already busy with activity. Ambrosia and Felicia were seated at the table across from the Doyles. The ladies were sipping tea and eating toast while Arnold Doyle had a rather mountainous plate filled with sausages, eggs, and fried bread.

A butter dish sat near Ambrosia, and Mr. Doyle nodded towards it. "Would you mind passing the butter, ma'am?"

Ambrosia blinked hard and Felicia passed the item across the table using the opportunity to explain, "Grandmama doesn't like being called 'ma'am.'"

"Felicia!" Ambrosia scolded.

"What's wrong with 'ma'am'?" Mr. Doyle said. His accent was definitely New York, but Ginger heard a twang of Irish resonating underneath.

Ambrosia narrowed her eyes and worked her wrinkled lips.

"It's what you call the Queen," Ginger said as she took a seat. "In polite society, we refer to a lady as madam, but you may address the dowager as Lady Gold."

Mr. Doyle guffawed and Ambrosia stared back, aghast.

Mrs. Doyle, being British herself, and somewhat of a timid mouse next to her boorish husband, blushed with mortification. "Please don't mind my husband," she said softly.

Ginger felt compelled to explain her relationship to Ambrosia and Felicia further. "My late husband, Daniel, was Lady Gold's grandson and Miss Gold's brother."

"Ah, that's why you feel like you have to let them live with you, huh?" Mr. Doyle said.

"Mr. Doyle, I do nothing under compulsion," Ginger said, "I assure you." Stepping to the sideboard, she let out a controlled breath. If the man didn't watch his manners he'd soon be out on his ear.

Basil arrived looking clean-shaven and dapper as ever, followed by Louisa and then Scout. Each new entry ignited a round of Happy or Merry Christmas greetings.

Boss sneaked in behind Scout and sat on his haunches behind Scout's chair. Ginger thought she was the only one who noticed that Scout was slipping the dog bits of his breakfast, but Arnold Doyle spotted it too.

"Does your dog do tricks, or does he get to eat for nothing?"

Scout glanced nervously between Ginger and Mr. Doyle. Ginger took pity on him. "Boss is very bright."

"Boss, huh? Clever."

"It's short for Boston."

"A reminder of home, I say. Does he do any tricks?"

Ginger nodded to Scout, giving him permission to demonstrate. Boss went through the usual dog tricks of "sit, roll over, beg, and play dead". Ginger knew her pet was capable of so much more, but he obliged obediently, satisfying Mr. Doyle's need to be entertained.

"And how did you teach him to do all that?" he asked.

"With peanut butter," Ginger said. "It's not available here in England, sadly, but Boss is quite fond of it and would do anything to gain a small taste as a reward."

"I don't eat nuts," Mr. Doyle said. "Nasty things. Meant for squirrels and birds, not men."

"They make him cough and wheeze," Mrs. Doyle added.

Mr. Doyle looked at Scout and smiled broadly. "Thank you for the show, son." He fished through his trouser pocket and retrieved an American penny, and offered it to Scout. "Your reward. Consider it a down payment for when you travel to America one day."

Ginger considered Arnold Doyle with surprise. The man had a thoughtful side after all.

Sally was the last to arrive, and when she entered the doorway, her eyes latched on the Doyles and she blanched.

"Hello, Arnold," she said. "I heard you and your wife would be joining my family for Christmas."

"Howdy, Sally, and a Merry Christmas to you."

Sally regained her composure. "Merry Christmas, everyone." Glancing briefly at Ruby Doyle she added, "Nice to see you again, Mrs. Doyle." She helped herself to a cup of coffee, sat in an empty chair opposite the Doyles, and spoke in soft tones with Louisa. Ginger found it rather interesting that, though Sally and the Doyles were obviously acquainted, she had no desire to engage in conversation with them beyond the unavoidable morning introductions. Ginger's curiosity was too great to let that pass.

"Sally, you and Mr. and Mrs. Doyle are acquainted through Father?"

Sally shot Ginger a withering look. "You already know that."

"I know, though the details are rather vague."

Sally cast a quick glance at the Doyles. "Arnold and George had business dealings."

"I did mention I was a friend of your father's," Mr. Doyle said. "Sally was never very fond of us."

Ambrosia nearly choked on her tea. Such provocation! Sally remained straight-faced, refusing a denial.

Ginger looked pointedly at Arnold and Ruby Doyle. "Will you be joining us for church this morning?"

"If you don't mind," Mrs. Doyle said. "It is Christmas."

"Of course we don't mind." Ginger would need to ring for a taxicab to facilitate the extra numbers.

. . .

THE REST of the morning went as planned. They politely opened gifts, then went to church. Everyone returned to Hartigan House reminded of their faith and the importance of goodwill, and, of course, frightfully hungry. The delectable scents of roast goose with all the trimmings drifted up from the kitchen and made their mouths water.

Everyone waited in the drawing room until the mid-afternoon meal was ready. A table with small savoury treats was set up to nibble on, along with a fully stocked drinks trolley.

The arrival of Basil's parents along with their aged friends Mr. and Mrs. Davenport came as expected. If all Ginger did was survive her new in-laws, the Honourable Henry and Mrs. Anna Reed, she would indeed deem the day a success. Unfortunately, Ginger had come up short on their expectations, having failed thus far and probably forever to produce a blood heir, and had added insult to injury by daring to adopt a lad who'd once lived on the streets. To add to the elder Reeds' disgruntlement, Basil had sided with Ginger, even on a threat of being removed from their will.

"So lovely to see you again," Basil said to the Davenports, giving each of them a hearty handshake.

Ginger stepped in behind Basil and did the same. "Such a pleasure to make your acquaintance," she said. "Happy Christmas!"

Mr. Davenport did the talking for his wife, who despite the joyous occasion failed to offer a single smile. Mrs. Davenport's hair was so white it looked blue, and her eyes, sunken in soft skin with plenty of folds, were devoid of emotion. Ginger wondered if perhaps the lady was beginning to suffer from dementia.

DR. AND MRS. GUPTA, a young, attractive couple, arrived, and Ginger welcomed them warmly. "So nice to see you again. Such a pleasure for us that you could attend."

The Guptas removed their coats and scarves, which were shuttled away by Pippins.

"The pleasure is ours," Dr. Gupta said. "It's the first time for my wife to experience the Christian celebration in England."

Mrs. Gupta's shiny black hair was knotted at the base of her neck and glistened under the electric lights.

"So different from India," she said. Though such a thing wasn't mentioned, Manu Gupta's wife was in the family way, and her rounded form could no longer be hidden, even under the straight-lined fashion of modern frocks.

They joined the others in the drawing room and introductions were made all around.

"The Davenports are long-time friends of the Reed family," Mr. Reed said. Basil's father was a handsome older man with grey hair and Basil's hazel eyes.

"We're friends with the Lester family as well," Mr. Davenport said. He considered Ruby Doyle with kind eyes. "You've been missed."

Ruby's gaze shot to her husband who watched her carefully. "It's very difficult, with my living in America now, to stay in touch."

Ginger thought the sentiment odd, since the post travelled regularly across the Atlantic now.

"We see your brother Alan now and again," Mr. Davenport added.

"I met Mr. Lester myself yesterday, at St. George's," Ginger said. "I've invited him for dinner."

"How nice." Mrs. Davenport remarked politely.

Mr. Doyle was less enthusiastic. "That's rather extraordinary," he said stiffly. Ginger got the impression Arnold Doyle didn't admire his brother-in-law. He stared at Ginger. "Did he know you'd be there?"

"Well, I suppose Reverend Hill may have mentioned it." Ginger wondered at the question, and more importantly, at the suspicion that laced Arnold Doyle's voice. Did he think Alan Lester had somehow planned the meeting and made a play to get himself invited?

"But he's more than welcome," Ginger added. "I found him to be very amiable." As had Felicia, who'd fancied him at first sight.

Mr. Doyle, for once, had nothing to say. The doorbell chimed almost at the same instant that Pippins came to announce that the Christmas meal was about to be served.

"That'll be Mr. Lester at the door," Ginger said. "Pips, please see him in."

THE FORMAL DINING room was rectangular in shape, and the long dining table, covered now with a white linen cloth, stretched out under a broad electric chandelier. Ladder back chairs with padded rose velvet seats encircled the table which was decorated with sprigs of holly and a number of candles in silver candlesticks flickering comforting light. The bone china plates held matching bowls and were paired with polished silver cutlery and crystal goblets. Ginger was delighted with the ambiance.

The guests were seated with Basil at one end and Ginger's chair at the other. To Basil's right sat Ambrosia, always upright and on the verge of becoming ruffled. At her side sat Mr. Davenport, his face tight with practiced propriety; following him the agreeable Mrs. Gupta, Mr. Doyle with his constant haughty grin, and Mrs. Reed, her eyes bright with pride for her son, Basil. Next to her was Felicia who smiled prettily, and at Ginger's elbow, Scout, scrubbed clean and with his defiant wheat-coloured hair poking up despite the hair oil, looking entirely uncomfortable in this posh company. To Basil's left sat Sally, whose stern expression spoke of something she had to endure rather than enjoy. Dr. Gupta with his kind smile sat next to Mrs. Davenport who blinked as if she'd forgotten who she was. Mr. Lester glanced about with his extraordinary eyes; beside him, Mrs. Doyle's gaze seemed to drift from her brother to her clasped palms on her lap. Mr. Reed sat tall with his usual confidence, and Louisa at Ginger's right seemed rather enthralled by the whole affair.

Ginger didn't miss how Felicia held Mr. Lester's gaze with a look of admiration, whilst Louisa, seated on the same side of the long table as the bachelor, had to strain her neck to get a better look at the handsome man. Oh mercy. There might be a battle for the poor man's attentions.

It was hard to miss the tension in the room, though Ginger was at a loss as to why it was there. Mr. Doyle glared at Mr. Lester, who was seated directly across the table from him, signalling that there was no love lost there. Ambrosia appeared lost seated between Basil and Mr. Davenport, and quite put out at having to face Sally for the entire meal. The Reeds were rather sour faced, though Ginger found they were generally like that in her presence as a rule, but in this moment, their animosity appeared to be directed at Mr. Doyle. Not only that, a wall of animosity also seemed to radiate across the table between Mr. Doyle and Sally. Arnold Doyle was certainly not a sympathetic character, and Ginger was left to wonder how on earth all these people had managed to end up at Hartigan House for Christmas dinner.

"Isn't this lovely?" Ginger proclaimed, in an effort to cut through the awkwardness with her charm. "Such a delight to have all of you to celebrate Christmas at Hartigan House. Mrs. Beasley has been labouring for days, and I'm sure we're all ready to eat. But first, I'm told we must uphold the English tradition of 'crackers'."

Lizzie produced a tray piled with tubular items decorated in colourful paper and tied at either end with matching bows.

Mr. Doyle burst out laughing. "In America, crackers are something to eat."

Mr. Davenport responded, "You'll find we have an entirely different lexicon on this side of the pond."

The crackers were distributed as Ginger explained the procedure for the sake of her American guests. "With arms crossed, take hold of one end of the cracker as your neighbour takes the other. On Basil's count, everyone pulls."

"What happens then?" Mr. Doyle asked.

"You'll see," Ginger said with a twinkle. Basil counted to three, and everyone pulled.

The sharp, snappy sound from his cracker made Mr. Doyle jump.

"What the dev-" he began, then his attention was drawn to the little toy whistle that had fallen out of the tube onto his plate. He picked it up and unwrapped the paper crown from around it.

"Are we really meant to put these silly hats on our heads?" Arnold Doyle bellowed. "That's *crackers.*" He laughed alone at his joke.

Ginger thought the tradition rather undignified, but placed the paper hat on her head as everyone else around the table did the same.

Scout, remaining silent as instructed, happily placed his paper hat on his head and produced a big toothy grin, then handled the miniature deck of cards his cracker had produced with delight. *If only we could all experience the simplicity of joy as a child,* Ginger thought.

Lizzie and Grace brought out silver bowls of oyster soup which was dished out and enjoyed. Then came the roast goose, the heavy platter carried out by Clement, Ginger's gardener and sometimes chauffer, already carved and ready. The maids presented trays of Brussels sprouts, roast potatoes, parsnips, apple sauce, and stuffing.

It was quite obvious to all but perhaps himself that Arnold Doyle delighted in being the centre of attention and was rather good at taking over the conversation. Ginger wondered if he even made note of the quieter ones around the table.

Mr. Doyle helped himself to another slice of roast goose along with what was left of the parsnips, but avoided the accompanying Brussels sprouts.

"Turkeys are the big thing in the United States, now, along with this thing called Jell-O," he said, while capturing a belch in his fist. "A jiggly gelatine affair, but not bad when it's sweetened."

Mrs. Ruby Doyle, an English rose through and through, blushed red with embarrassment at her husband's obtuse nature and rather gluttonous behaviour, though she kept a stiff upper lip, as the Brits were wont to say, and stared blankly across the table.

Her brother, Alan Lester, frowned in Doyle's direction. "We've heard of both turkeys and gelatine on this side of the pond."

Dr. Gupta and Mr. Davenport carried on a polite conversation across the table, having discovered they both shared an interest in physics.

"Siegbahn deserved his Nobel Prize win," Mr. Davenport said.

"Indeed," Dr. Gupta agreed. "To think what great use to modern medicine his discoveries in the field of X-ray spectroscopy will be."

Mr. Reed raised a glass in a toast. "To our host and hostess, Basil and Ginger."

Glasses were tapped together and tinkled all around.

"Thank you," Basil said. "My wife and I wish each one of you a happy Christmas and prosperous 1926."

"Hear, hear," Mr. Davenport said. "To a jolly good new year. Any plans to waste on it?"

"Only to continue serving the city in my capacity at the Yard," Basil said.

"I'll be staying close to home," Dr. Gupta said. He glanced lovingly at his bride who simply glowed, Ginger thought, with a baby due soon. The couple's family lived in India and so they had happily accepted Ginger's invitation to the Christmas celebration when she offered it. Ginger and Dr. Gupta's paths crossed often and she considered him a friend.

"I've got plans to go abroad," Mr. Lester said. He wistfully looked at his sister. "I wish you could come with me."

"What?" Mr. Doyle's voice reverberated to the high ceiling, and Ginger thought that it might be time to slow down on the wine refills.

Ruby quickly raised a palm in her husband's direction. "He's not being literal."

"She's right," Mr. Lester said stiffly. "It's only a dream."

Felicia had been casting glances across the table at Alan Lester all evening. "Where are you going, Mr. Lester?" she asked.

Mr. Lester, moving away from his serious demeanour, spoke with a flirtatious lilt. "Australia,

Miss Gold. Perhaps, since my sister is indisposed, you'd be interested in an adventure." He caught Ginger's disapproving eye and added, "Chaperoned, of course."

Felicia giggled. "I wish! I've never been off this dismal island. Not even to France! How I'd love a bit of sunshine."

Ambrosia looked thoroughly ill at ease. She muttered something to herself; Ginger, watching her lips, thought it might have been, "I'm not sure how many more Christmas dinners I can bear."

Arnold Doyle dropped a napkin onto his empty plate. "What we need now is a big piece of chocolate cake."

Ginger held her tongue. Mr. Doyle's rudeness was beyond acknowledging. One simply didn't dictate the menu to one's host.

"It's tradition in England, Mr. Doyle," Ginger said calmly, "to serve plum pudding after the Christmas meal."

"Pudding? From plums?"

"It's not pudding in the way that Americans define the word," Ginger said. She'd spent twenty years living in Boston and was quite familiar with the milk-based sweet. "Pudding in England is another word for dessert. More like the American cake."

"I jest, Mrs. Reed. I'm Irish, remember. I know what plum pudding is, though I can't say I've missed it."

As if on cue, Lizzie pushed through the swinging door, presenting a heavy platter on which perched a half-sphere-shaped cake decorated with a sprig of holly, ablaze in blue flames which licked all over it.

Though everyone around the table was familiar with the event, they couldn't keep *oohs* and *aahs* from escaping their lips.

The platter was set in front of Ginger who quickly sliced the dessert and passed the pieces around the table. With so many in attendance, it required quite a finesse to ensure each one's piece still had a flame licking it.

"Make your wishes, everyone!" Ginger proclaimed. A period of silence followed, and Ginger wished dreadfully that for that one moment in time, she could read minds.

She picked up the crystal dish of brandy sauce that Pippins had placed in front of her, put only a small spoonful of the stiff white cream on Scout's piece of pudding, since it did have alcohol in it, a larger dollop for herself, then passed it along.

"Brandy's the best part of the whole thing," Mr. Doyle declared when the bowl reached him, and he added a generous amount to his portion. He took a bite. "Not bad for something that's been on fire."

"It's basically fruit cake," Sally answered. "I was married to an Englishman for many years. I'm no stranger to plum pudding, but like you, Mr. Doyle, I don't understand what all the fuss is about."

"It's tradition," Ginger said. She'd been raised in Boston, but still these two Americans made her feel that she needed to come to the defence of her British heritage.

"It's got nothing on chocolate cake," Mr. Doyle replied. He picked something out of his teeth. "What's this? Oh, look, a sixpence!"

Scout stared down the table in shock. "There's money in the pudding?"

"Yes, Scout," Ginger said with a smile. "Perhaps you'd like to finish yours now?"

Scout dug around on his plate until his spoon hit something hard. "I found one!" His smile crumpled. "It's only a button."

Ginger chuckled. "That means you'll stay a bachelor this year."

Mr. Lester appealed to Ginger. "I hope you don't mind that I didn't touch mine. I mean, after I added the brandy butter."

"It's quite all right," Ginger said lightly. "But you'll never know what you might've lost out on."

Mr. Lester pushed the pudding to the middle of the table in front of him.

Mr. Doyle raised a bushy brow. "If you don't want it?"

Mr. Lester shrugged. "Be my guest."

Mr. Doyle chuckled. "I never say no to free money."

"Lizzie," Ginger said before her helpful and patient maid departed. "I think we'll be ready for coffee in the drawing room soon."

"Yes, madam. I'll tell Mrs. Beasley."

Ginger's attention was captured by the trilling panic of Ruby Doyle's voice. "Arnold? *Arnold?*"

Mr. Arnold Doyle was grabbing at his throat, making gurgling sounds as his thick tongue protruded from his mouth and his face turned purple. Had he accidentally swallowed his coin?

"Dr. Gupta!" Ginger turned to Manu Gupta who was already on his feet, rushing from his place on the opposite side of the table.

Before the doctor could respond to Arnold Doyle's distress, the man grew limp and his head fell forward, his face landing firmly in what remained of his pudding.

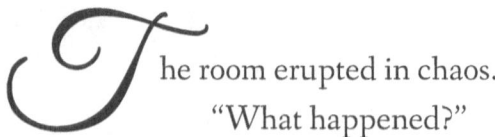he room erupted in chaos.

"What happened?"

"Is he dead?"

Ruby Doyle rushed around the table, shoved at her husband's shoulders, and screamed. "Arnold!"

"Give the medical man space," Basil instructed.

Dr. Gupta lifted Arnold Doyle's bloated face and lowered his ear to listen for breath. He frowned and placed two fingers at the man's throat, then stared back at Ginger and shook his head.

Ambrosia grasped the collar of her blouse. "Dear Lord."

Ruby covered her face, now red and tight as she desperately tried to hold in a sob.

"He choked to death?" Alan Lester said, eyes wide with disbelief.

"Oh, Ginger!" Louisa squealed. "Might I be excused? This is just too ghastly."

"Yes, of course," Ginger said. To Felicia she said, "Would you mind taking Scout to his room?"

"But, Mum," Scout said, "this is jolly excitin'." Ginger cast him a surprised look. It was the first time Scout had resisted her in any way. It actually made Ginger's heart leap. As her ward, Scout had always obeyed, as if he were a servant, but just now, he sounded like a *son*.

"This is no place for children," she said. "Now run along."

Mrs. Davenport slumped in her chair, fainting.

"Mary!" Mr. Davenport said.

"I'll get smelling salts," Ginger said. By now Pippins and Lizzie had heard the commotion and arrived.

"I'll get them, madam," Lizzie said.

Anna Reed, who'd been sitting beside Mr. Doyle, had long since scurried away from the dead man and hovered behind her husband's chair.

Henry Reed snapped at Basil, "Do something."

Basil, who was already on his feet, said, "Do

remain calm. Pippins, please escort everyone to the drawing room."

"Make use of the drinks trolley," Ginger added, certain that everyone could use a little something to calm their nerves.

"Now I wish I hadn't given Langley the day off," Ambrosia said. She pressed against her walking stick and rose. "I need to lie down."

"Grace can assist you," Ginger offered. Ambrosia waved her off.

"I'm quite capable of doing the stairs on my own. I'm not an invalid yet."

Lizzie arrived with the smelling salts. Mr. Davenport took them from her hand, held them under his wife's nose, and watched her stir back to consciousness.

"Please summon my driver," he said to the maid. Then he turned to Ginger. "You'll excuse us for leaving early, Mrs. Reed, due to the circumstances?"

"I understand," Ginger said. "Pippins, please assist the Davenports with whatever they need."

Ginger and Basil pulled Dr. Gupta aside and they spoke quietly together.

"Cause of death?" Basil asked

"It appears that man simply choked," Dr. Gupta

said. "I would've considered poison as a possibility, but we all ate of the same pudding."

"How unfortunate," Ginger murmured. She stared with empathy at Ruby who was slumped in her chair and being awkwardly comforted by her brother. Christmas Day would forever be marred for the new widow.

"Perhaps I should take Ruby home with me," Alan Lester said when he noticed Ginger watching. "Such a shock."

"I'm afraid I have to ask everyone to remain for the time being," Basil said with a note of authority. "With all cases of sudden death, it's police procedure to take statements. If everyone would please return to the drawing room and await my further instructions."

"But, surely, this is accidental," Mr. Davenport said. "And my wife—"

Ginger jumped in. "If you and Mrs. Davenport would prefer a quiet room of your own, Pippins can show you to the library."

Mr. Davenport blew out his jowls. "That's unnecessary. We don't need special treatment."

Dr. Gupta excused himself to use the telephone. "I'll arrange for an ambulance to pick up the body."

"What do you think?" Ginger said to Basil once the dining room had cleared out.

"It's quite likely accidental, but one thing I've learned from my years on the force is that things are rarely what they seem."

6

Ginger's household kept Boxing Day—the twenty-sixth of December—according to the tradition of boxing up leftover food and treats for the servants. She had given all her staff the rest of the day off after the breakfast buffet was set up, with permission to take whatever remainders they liked, along with a wrapped gift of new gloves for each.

After the uproar of the day before, the house was quiet, with only Ginger and Basil enjoying their breakfast together in relative silence. Felicia and Louisa, still young enough to master having a lie-in, had yet to arrive in the morning room, while early risers Ambrosia and Scout had already been and gone. Ginger wasn't sure what Sally was up to.

The radio played behind them and a news broadcaster turned to international news. *White Hand Gang leader Richard 'Pegleg' Lonergan was killed early on Boxing Day.*

Basil perked up. "That's the Irish mafia, isn't it?"

Ginger nodded and kept listening.

Lonergan, along with five of his men, arrived at a Christmas party in a Brooklyn speakeasy. Al Capone was in the club and it's speculated that he had the killing arranged.

"Crime doesn't stop for Christmas," Ginger said, then went on to change the subject.

"I still feel terrible about last night. My guests expected an evening of relaxation and joy and instead got the shock of their lives." With short meal and tea breaks, the interviews had gone on towards midnight, and by the time everyone had either left or gone to bed, the well-wishing wasn't Happy Christmas or Goodnight, but *Please don't leave town.* After a sip of coffee she added, "And poor Arnold Doyle. His face as he—"

Basil nodded as he chewed a piece of sausage. "What do you know about the man, exactly?"

Ginger had already relayed everything she knew, but didn't mind going over it again. Speaking aloud often brought more clarity.

"He had business dealings with my father, I'm not sure what, but according to Sally, I was still in my teens. Mr. Doyle inferred in our correspondence that his relationship with my father had been amiable, but Sally doesn't remember it that way."

"Mrs. Hartigan doesn't seem to remember much," Basil said.

Ginger recalled the uncomfortable interview she and Basil had had with her the night before. If Ginger hadn't known better, she would've thought her stepmother guilty of something. The way the muscles around her mouth tightened when she talked, her vague responses, and her apparent inability to look them in the eye all hinted at a secret.

If Sally Hartigan harboured guilt, Ginger couldn't imagine what it would be for; and how it could be connected to Mr. Doyle's death was a further mystery.

Mrs. Doyle hadn't been much better, though Ginger could excuse her inability to cooperate through shock and grief.

"Arnold Doyle certainly came across as a man who was used to getting what he wanted," Basil said. "The question is what had he wanted?"

"Whatever it was brought him to London," Ginger said. "But why contact me? Why request to stay at Hartigan House when there are plenty of hotels in the city? Why the ruse about his friendship with my father?"

"Perhaps he was on the run," Basil suggested. "He might've burned his bridges in America. Tracking him to a hotel may have been too easy, or perhaps he felt he could protect himself more easily if he stayed away from a public setting."

"That's rather unnerving," Ginger said. "He might've brought trouble to our family."

Basil grunted. "Mr. Doyle didn't behave like a man who gave the welfare of others much thought. I'll do some digging, see what I can find about his history."

"Can you do that?" Ginger asked. "No crime has been committed."

"That we know of." Basil refilled his coffee cup from the pot sitting on the table. "Think about all the people around the table who might've had something against the deceased, beginning with his worn-down wife, Ruby. It must've been hard for her brother, Alan, to watch it."

"Ruby mentioned Alan was her only sibling," said Ginger.

"The Davenports were family friends of the Lesters, and Mr. Davenport seemed offended by the man's existence." Basil sighed. "And I regret having to add Sally to the list, but she was also acquainted through your father with Mr. Doyle."

Ginger hated to think that Sally could be involved in anything insidious. And besides, Mr. Doyle's death hadn't been ruled suspicious.

Yet.

GINGER CALLED on Boss to join her on her benevolent visit to the bereaved at Alan Lester's residence. His presence often softened an otherwise tense meeting.

"Give my regards," Basil said. His hazel eyes twinkled with understanding. Ginger didn't have to come out and say that she wasn't merely about to extend her sympathies once again, but was in need of satisfying her curiosity. How were brother and sister handling the sudden death of an aggressive family member?

It was a lovely drive through Hyde Park, though a number of large puddles caused Ginger to yank on the large steering wheel, nearly hitting a horse and carriage. The city streets were better and before long, Ginger arrived in the area where Alan Lester lived in one of a row of townhouses.

Neither rich nor poor, Mr. Lester lived comfortably, however, he didn't employ a butler, and opened the door to Ginger's knock himself.

He frowned when he saw her, and Ginger suspected it wasn't solely because of Boss whose dark head stuck out of the crook of her arm.

"Mrs. Reed?"

"Please do forgive my calling like this," Ginger said, "but I've come to see how you and Mrs. Doyle are faring today. I feel a modicum of responsibility since the occasion of your unhappiness occurred whilst you were guests in my home."

Mr. Lester was too much of a gentleman to let Ginger stand on the doorstep in the cold wind.

"I hope you don't mind that I've brought my dog," she said. "He's very well trained and I'll keep him on my lap. You won't even notice he's with me."

"It's fine," Mr. Lester said. "Ruby and I grew up with animals."

Ginger followed him inside the house and into the sitting room.

Ruby Doyle sat in a high-backed chair that faced the window, and was having breakfast on a tray.

"I'm interrupting," Ginger said.

"Nonsense," Mr. Lester said. "We haven't even poured our tea yet. I'll fetch another teacup."

Ruby looked up at Ginger, her eyes widening. "Good morning, Mrs. Reed. Do have a seat."

"I hope you don't mind," Ginger said. "I'm just so very concerned about you. I couldn't imagine if something so dreadfully unexpected ever happened like that to my Basil."

Ginger had to tell herself not to come on too strong.

"It's a shock," Mrs. Doyle agreed. "Arnold was larger than life, as you saw. His presence filled a room. Life will seem so dull without him."

Ruby Doyle poured the tea into cups each with a little bit of milk in the bottom.

Ginger added a teaspoon of sugar to hers and stirred it with a tiny silver spoon. "What will you do now?" she asked.

Ruby held her teacup and saucer in front of her. "I don't know. I have a home in America, but my family is here. I think I'll probably go back to settle my affairs and return to London when it's done. Alan has kindly offered to let me live here with him, at least until I'm settled."

Alan Lester entered with the third tea setting and took a seat. "My home is her home."

"Will you go back alone?" Ginger asked. She had travelled the Atlantic by steamship more than once and it could be a long, lonely trip on one's own, especially if the weather was poor and storms rocked the boat.

"I'll go with her," Alan said. "As soon as the ticket office opens tomorrow morning, I'll ring to let them know what's happened."

Mrs. Doyle put a thin hand over one of Alan Lester's. "It's dangerous."

"More for you than me."

"How so?" Ginger asked.

The Lester siblings looked at Ginger as if they'd momentarily forgotten she was there.

"She's just worried about the trip over," Alan Lester said. "I've never been to America and I hate travelling by boat. I'm a poor swimmer, you see?"

Ginger smiled. "The steamship is so large, you'll hardly have to worry about going overboard." Her words were meant to comfort, but she couldn't help wonder how Mr. Lester had planned to go to Australia if not by ship. What of his water phobia, then?

7

*G*inger made an impromptu decision to call
in on Mr. and Mrs. Davenport. Not long
ago, Mrs. Davenport had had a gown
made at Feathers & Flair and Ginger recalled the
address where the item had been delivered.

Mr. Davenport's animosity toward Arnold Doyle
had hardly been disguised, and Ginger hoped to get
to the bottom of the reason why. A long row of
motorcars was already parked in front of the Mayfair
townhouse where the Davenports resided and
Ginger claimed a spot down the way, only just
tapping the lamppost with her front bumper.

"They really should've set those farther apart on
the pavement," Ginger said to Boss. The rain had

increased in its intensity, and Ginger popped open an umbrella as she stepped out of the Crossley. Boss watched her with bright round eyes.

"Perhaps you should wait this one out," Ginger said to him. "It's damp for your feet, and I'm not sure Mrs. Davenport would approve. I shan't be long."

Boss, accepting his fate, remained on his haunches as Ginger closed the door. Ginger took a moment to examine the latest scratch on her poor Crossley, a bright wound, glossy from the rain. Had Ginger not moved her umbrella at just the right moment, she would've missed the exit of a lady from the Davenports' door. Ginger gasped and stepped away from her distinctive vehicle, keeping the edge of her umbrella tilted just so, in order to protect her identity.

Once the coast was clear, Ginger, keeping in step with the other pedestrians on the pavement who were clearly more relaxed during the festive season than Ginger was feeling, approached the Davenports' front door and knocked. A butler answered.

"Good morning," Ginger said as she handed over her card.

The butler waved her into the hall and out of the rain. "Please wait a moment, madam."

When the butler returned, Ginger followed him

down a short corridor to a set of open birch-wood doors. Mr. and Mrs. Davenport were seated in chairs facing the roaring fire.

Mr. Davenport got to his feet and approached with an outstretched arm. "Welcome, Mrs. Reed."

Ginger shook his meaty palm with her gloved hand. "Please forgive my calling unannounced," Ginger said with a warm smile. "I was in the area and decided to take the chance that you were at home. I'm so dreadfully sorry about the shocking event that occurred yesterday in my home and I wanted to make certain that you both were well."

Mrs. Davenport offered a weak smile. "You're always welcome, Mrs. Reed." To the butler she said, "Jones, please arrange for tea."

Ginger took the proffered seat, a third chair Mr. Davenport had slid in between his and his wife's.

"The weather is ghastly," Ginger said. Nothing like talk of the weather to break the ice. "I thought the fog was bad, but now with the rain, it's a hazard to drive at all."

"Jolly good that you came to us, then," Mr. Davenport said. "Until the weather breaks, we wouldn't want you to take unnecessary risks on the road."

The butler returned with the tray and set it on

the tea table in front of Mrs. Davenport. She asked, "Milk, Mrs. Reed?"

"Thank you, yes," Ginger said.

A moment passed while they sipped their tea and watched the flames shoot and dodge up the chimney.

"Do you have plans to bring in the new year?" Ginger asked. "I can hardly believe it's almost 1926."

Mr. Davenport glanced at his wife. "We're undecided at the moment," he said. "What would you suggest?"

"My family and I are attending the ball at the Ritz. There's going to be an orchestra and dancing. I can see that invitations are extended."

Mrs. Davenport looked up over her teacup. "It sounds lovely."

Ginger felt a pang of concern for her hostess. She was like a beautiful fern that had been left without water for too long. If Ginger was going to get the answers she wanted, she felt she'd better get to it. She cleared her throat and began.

"I hate to bring up such a frightfully distasteful subject as Mr. Doyle's death, but in case there's an inquiry, I must make note of all the details, and since you were present, I have a few questions."

Mr. Davenport's chin jerked upwards. "Why would there be an inquiry? The cause of death was accidental, was it not?"

"It actually hasn't been officially determined," Ginger replied. "With Christmas, everything is closed and delayed." She smiled as benignly as possible. "I like to be prepared."

Mrs. Davenport's hand shook as she lowered her teacup and saucer to the occasional table beside her. "Forgive me, Mrs. Reed, I'm feeling rather under the weather. I hope you don't mind my husband's company for the time being?"

"Not at all," Ginger said. "I do hope you feel better soon."

After watching his wife leave the room, Mr. Davenport let out a long sigh.

"We lost both of our sons in the war, and now there'll be no grandchildren, you see? She's never quite recovered."

"I'm so very sorry for your losses," Ginger said sincerely. "My first husband died near the end. It was a dreadful time."

"So many of us had reason to grieve. It's been seven years, and yet, at times, it feels like we only heard the horrible news yesterday."

Mr. Davenport emptied his teacup.

Ginger lifted the teapot. "Mr. Davenport?"

He nodded and Ginger poured for both of them.

"Did you know Mr. Doyle?" Ginger asked. "From before Christmas day?"

Mr. Davenport stirred sugar into his cup and made a show of a taking a slow sip, his gaze calculating how to respond. Ginger held her breath, hoping for the truth.

She was to be disappointed.

"No, no," he finally said. "How could I? I've never been to New York in my life."

"I see," Ginger said. "I only thought you might've, since you appeared rather astonished to see him there."

"I was astonished by his abrasive personality. His behaviour was an affront to an English gentleman."

Ginger considered Mr. Davenport as he relaxed back into his chair. Perhaps she had misjudged the man.

"Mr. Doyle was definitely a force of nature." Ginger set her unfinished tea aside. "I'll infringe on your hospitality no longer," she said. "I'm certain you're eager to see to Mrs. Davenport."

Mr. Davenport walked Ginger to the front door.

"Have you had any other guests today?" Ginger asked, conversationally, thinking of the lady she'd seen leave just moments before she herself had arrived. "Christmas well-wishers?"

Mr. Davenport's expression went blank. "The day's been rather uneventful, Mrs. Reed. We do thank you for lighting it up a little."

"Happy New Year, Mr. Davenport," Ginger said. She ducked under her umbrella, grateful the intensity of the rain had lifted, and returned carefully to her motorcar.

Boss greeted her with puppy-like enthusiasm and she patted him on the head. "I've learned a couple of interesting new facts, Bossy. Sally Hartigan visited the Davenports just before I did, and Mr. Davenport lied about it. Now why would he do that?"

THE FESTIVE WEEKEND ended and Scotland Yard was back in business. Basil kissed Ginger goodbye before leaving early in the morning to "tackle a tower of paperwork". Ginger thought it would be prudent to make an appearance at her Regent Street dress shop, Feathers & Flair, though a quick telephone call to Madame Roux had calmed her. "Zee shop is ready, but customers are few," the shop manager had said. "I vill ring you if it changes."

Ginger had completed her orders for factory frocks and imported fabrics before Christmas Eve, and all the gowns on order for the festive season had been delivered. Things were sure to get busy again in the new year with spring on the horizon, but for now, Ginger decided she should enjoy the quiet.

Perhaps a ride on Goldmine was in order. The weather was sunny but cold, with a bank of clouds threatening on the horizon.

Scout was thrilled at the prospect of riding Sir Blackwell, and they both changed quickly into their riding outfits.

The house was comparatively calm, with Basil back to work, Ambrosia knitting in the sitting room, and Felicia and Louisa out and about, bound for some sort of mischief. Once again Sally was unaccounted for, and Ginger was glad she'd asked Clement to discreetly follow her wayward stepmother. It was because of this that she was surprised to encounter her gardener as she headed for the stable. He approached when he spotted her.

To Scout Ginger said, "Go on. I'll only be a minute."

"Clement? I thought you were *running an errand.*"

Clement stood closely, his head turned away from the windows of Hartigan House, as if someone inside could possibly read his lips. Ginger was amused by how seriously the man took this task, and yet, here he stood, unmoved.

"Madam, I'm doin' as you asked. Mrs. Hartigan is in the stable with the 'orses.". Clement tapped his wristwatch. "She's been inside for sixteen minutes."

Ginger wrinkled her brow at this odd discovery. If there was one thing she knew about Sally, it was that she didn't like the smell of horses.

"You're sure she hasn't come out?"

"Quite sure, madam."

"Thank you, Clement. That will be all for now."

Ginger found Scout and Sally inside the stable, at opposite ends to each other, staring with narrowed eyes, each suspicious of the other.

Hartigan House, which was located on Mallowan Court in South Kensington, just south of Kensington Gardens, was surrounded by a considerable amount of land for a London property. A stone stable sat beside the motorcar garage, and the scent of hay, horses, and a hint of manure tickled Ginger's senses as she approached.

"Scout, love," Ginger said. "I forgot to take Boss for a short walk. Would you mind fetching him and taking him around the court?"

Scout wrinkled his small upturned nose at the change of plans. "And then we'll ride?"

"Yes, then we'll ride," Ginger said. "I promise."

Scout left, a skip in his step, since his disappointment at the delay was quickly overshadowed by the affection he had for the little Boston terrier.

Ginger approached Goldmine, stroked his neck, and then turned to Sally who'd remained in her position standing beside a hay bale. "Is everything all right, Sally?"

Something flashed behind Sally's eyes, a plea of sorts, or perhaps fear? Ginger's stepmother was a fortress, and, with the exception of the day that they'd lowered George Hartigan into the ground, Ginger couldn't remember Sally ever looking vulnerable or afraid. "If something's the matter," Ginger said kindly, "you can tell me."

Sally's mouth opened, and for a brief moment Ginger thought she'd confide in her. But then her lips snapped shut and her eyes darkened. She shifted off the hay bale and brushed hay residue from her pleated green and brown woollen skirt.

"I thought maybe I'd like to ride, that's all. It's a

little too chilly for my liking," she said with a brusque Boston accent and headed for the stable door. "I didn't mean to interrupt your plans, Ginger. You shouldn't have been so quick to chase your stable boy away."

Sally knew Scout wasn't a mere stable boy, but Ginger let the dig go. One had to choose one's battles, especially over the Christmas season, it seemed.

After Sally had left, Ginger picked up the brush and began the process of getting Goldmine saddled up. "She's up to something," she said to the gelding as she stroked his glossy mane.

Scout returned and before long they were riding the horses to Kensington Gardens. Ginger had such a pleasant time on the ride with her adopted son, she even forgot to think about the Doyle situation until after they were back and she'd changed out of her riding breeches.

Basil returned to Hartigan House with a frown and a wrinkled forehead. He was in the company of Constable Brian Braxton, a rather dapper young police officer who worked for Scotland Yard out of a sense of duty rather than financial need and had caught Felicia's eye. The fact that Braxton wore his uniform told Ginger this wasn't a social call.

"What is it, Basil?"

"I've heard from Dr. Gupta," Basil said. "Arnold Doyle's cause of death wasn't choking. It appears he may have been poisoned. I'm officially declaring his death suspicious."

8

Ginger beckoned to her faithful butler. "Pips, please let Mrs. Beasley, Lizzie, and Grace know that Mr. Reed would like to speak to them shortly."

Pippins bowed slightly. "Yes, madam."

Ginger rarely questioned Basil's intuition, but she had to ask, "Surely you don't think one of our staff had anything to do with Mr. Doyle's demise?"

"It's a matter of form, darling. I have to begin my inquiries somewhere, and since the plum pudding originated in the kitchen, it's prudent to start there."

Ginger had to agree and followed Basil and Constable Braxton to the kitchen. She heard the soft clicking of Boss' nails on the marble and grinned at her companion who'd decided to join them. Perhaps he hoped for a treat.

The kitchen was a wide, open square with plenty of shelving, a large gas stove, and a deep porcelain sink. A massive wooden table took up the centre of the room and overhead hung pots and pans of various sizes, along with sprigs of dried herbs.

Mrs. Beasley worried thick fingers in the fabric of her cotton apron, whilst Lizzie and Grace stood like slender poles on either side of her, as if they needed the rotund woman's protection.

"You may be at ease," Ginger said, stepping around Basil. "We've only a few questions."

Basil briefly stiffened as Ginger took over, but then relaxed. This wasn't unfamiliar territory between the pair, and Ginger had a way of making people comfortable when being questioned, which usually worked in Basil's favour. He let her proceed without interruption.

"As you know, a tragedy occurred during Christmas dinner, no fault of any of you, I'm sure, but sadly, it's come to our attention that Mr. Doyle's death wasn't accidental."

Mrs. Beasley's doughy hand flew to her mouth. "No, madam. That can't be so."

"I'm afraid it is. In this light, please cooperate fully with Mr. Reed's enquiries."

Basil stepped forward, nodding towards Ginger, as if accepting a baton.

"Mrs. Beasley," he began. "Who made the plum pudding?"

"I did, sir," the cook said. "I kept with tradition as much as possible, allowing members of the house-hold to give the pudding a stir, whoever wanted to. That would include us here in the room, Miss Gold and, er, Master Scout."

Ginger gave Mrs. Beasley credit for using Scout's new title, though it was clearly a challenge for the woman. It wasn't normal for a member of the serving class to rise in the ranks.

"And the ingredients?" Basil said. "Where did they come from?"

"Same place as always. The grocer's and the boy who brings the fruit and vegetables around."

Constable Braxton was taking notes and lifted his helmet-covered head. "Did anyone complain about the taste of the pudding?"

Ginger and Basil glanced at the constable sharply, and the younger officer looked back sheep-ishly, "I just thought, if someone had poisoned it, one might've noticed."

"Except that everyone would've become ill or worse," Basil said, "had the entire pudding been tampered with."

"Yes, sir, of course."

"And we don't know yet that the cause of death was poison," Ginger added. They only knew for certain that Mr. Doyle hadn't choked to death. They had to wait for laboratory tests before Dr. Gupta could confirm results.

Basil returned his attention to the kitchen staff. "I don't suppose the rubbish is still around. With the celebrations and everything? Maybe out the back?"

Mrs. Beasley's soft cheeks jiggled as she shook her head. "We always clean up every night and Clement takes the rubbish out the back."

"Mrs. Beasley," Basil started, "can you recall anyone else stepping into the kitchen who maybe shouldn't have been there?"

Mrs. Beasley glanced uncomfortably in Ginger's direction.

"It's all right," Ginger said. "You can answer the question."

Mrs. Beasley had made a tight knot of her apron by this point. "Very well, madam," she said. "It was Mrs. Hartigan. She came in when she thought I wasn't looking, my back turned to the door as I made the brandy butter."

GINGER'S HEART squeezed at the implication. She and Sally had never truly bonded, and Ginger viewed her more as a mother-figure than a person she could ever call "Mom", but despite their differences and rocky relationship, Sally Hartigan was family. She was Ginger's sister's mother and had been her father's wife.

Could she also be a murderer?

"We'll need to talk to Sally and Louisa," Basil said, once they were in the corridor and out of hearing range of the kitchen.

Sighing, Ginger said, "I'll ask Pippins to gather them in the sitting room."

Ginger waited with Basil on the settee whilst Constable Braxton stood at the ready by the door, helmet in hand. Ginger thought about inviting him to take a seat, but then, if Basil wanted his constable to relax he'd have done it himself.

The door finally swung open with the flamboyant entrance of Louisa. "Sister?" she said with a wave of theatrics. "You require my presence?"

Instead of Sally following behind, Felicia

entered. "Such a dreadfully grey morning! I'm so grateful for the Christmas party at Alison's tonight. It'll be dull compared to the Ritz, but still, a party is a party."

Everyone in the room, including Louisa, had noticed Constable Braxton stationed to the right of the door. Felicia, noticing that her audience was staring not at her, but past her, turned.

"Constable Braxton!" Her delight at seeing the young officer was evident in the rosy patches that highlighted her high cheekbones. "It's been ages!"

"Good day, Miss Gold."

Louisa, never one to be left out of anything, had scurried to Felicia's side. "Oh, who is this handsome charmer? Felicia, you must stop keeping all the handsome fellas to yourself."

Felicia shot Louisa a look of reproach, but then smiled at Brian Braxton. "Constable Braxton, this is Mrs. Reed's half-sister, Miss Louisa Hartigan. Louisa, this is my friend, Constable Braxton."

Constable Braxton shook Louisa's outstretched hand. "How do you do?"

"Simply fabulous now," Louisa said.

Ginger and Basil stared at each other with incredulousness. Basil cleared his throat.

"Ladies, Constable Braxton and I are here in an official capacity."

"We need to speak to Louisa and Sally at this time," Ginger said. "Felicia darling, would you mind looking for Sally and telling her that's she's needed?"

"Of course," Felicia said, though she frowned as her eyes passed from Brian Braxton to Louisa, who'd been grinning unashamedly in the young officer's direction.

Oh mercy, Ginger thought, thoroughly grateful that she had found Basil and was beyond the stage where one is constantly performing some sort of mating dance in search of love.

"You won't mind if I ring for tea," Louisa said. "I'm simply parched."

"Not at all," Ginger said.

Louisa rang the bell and soon Lizzie entered, curtsied, and asked, "What may I do for you, madam?"

"Please, Lizzie," Ginger started, "tea for us all. Thank you."

Louisa chose a chair that was angled towards the back of the room and crossed her legs, revealing calves covered in flesh-coloured silk stockings. She twisted a strand of her dark bob around a long finger and tilted her head back, her eyes remaining on the constable.

Such cheek! Ginger thought.

"Louisa, darling, if we could have your attention," she said. "Basil has a few questions."

The request forced Louisa to turn her back to the poor constable. She pouted, but complied. "Very well. What is it that you want to ask me?"

"Did you or your mother know Mr. and Mrs. Doyle prior to their arrival here?"

"I've never met them before in my life."

"How about their names?" Basil asked. "Did your mother or your father, before he passed away, ever mention them?"

"If they did, I wasn't aware of it." Louisa narrowed her eyes as her gaze darted between them. "Now, what's this about? You don't seriously think we had anything to do with the deplorable man's death? Just because he was American doesn't mean we'd know him."

Ginger replied, "It's simply a matter of procedure, Louisa. We got word that Mr. Doyle's death is suspicious so we have to make enquiries of everyone who was present."

"I don't see how I can be of any more help."

Felicia knocked lightly, but stepped in without

waiting to be asked. "Sorry to interrupt, but I thought you'd like to know that I can't find Mrs. Hartigan anywhere. She's not upstairs in her room or the library, nor the drawing room, dining room, or morning room on this floor. I've even checked your office, Ginger."

"What about in the back garden, or the stable?"

"I checked with Clement. She's not there, and none of the staff have seen her. It's like she's disappeared into thin air."

Pippins stepped in behind Felicia. "I'm afraid it's true, madam," he said to Ginger. "She's not on the property."

Basil caught Ginger's eye and asked, "Do you have a photograph of your stepmother?"

"I have a family album in my study, but surely she's not in danger? Quite likely she simply slipped out for a walk unnoticed."

"Without bothering to mention it to anyone?" Felicia asked, nosing in. "And the weather's nasty. Mrs. Hartigan doesn't strike me as the walking kind."

"She walks when it suits her," Louisa said sullenly. "It wouldn't be unlike Mother to think only of herself."

Ginger thought her sister's comment uncharitable, however, she was probably masking her own sense of fear with anger.

Basil got to his feet and waved Constable Braxton over.

"Sir?"

"Once Mrs. Reed procures a photograph of Mrs. Hartigan, take it to the station and ask the officers to search for her."

"Starting where, sir?"

"Just to keep a lookout on their beats. Like Mrs. Reed said, she's likely just doing a bit of shopping. And please let me know as soon as any information arrives regarding Mr. Doyle's background check."

"Yes, sir."

Ginger hurried to her study to retrieve the photo album tucked away on one of the bookshelves. She flipped it open to a photo of her father and Sally. It was one of the last photographs taken when her father was alive, sitting with all the dignity he could muster in a wooden wheelchair with a tartan wool blanket over bony legs. Sally stood stoically to his side, neither touching her husband nor his chair. Ginger lifted the photograph from the corner attachments and removed it.

She found Constable Braxton waiting in the

entrance, without Felicia and Louisa fluttering about him this time.

"Here you go," she said to the constable as she handed him the photograph. "I do hope you won't be needing it for long."

"As do I, madam." Constable Braxton fastened the strap of his helmet under his chin, nodded to Ginger, and left. "I'll make sure it gets back to you."

"I'm sure it's much ado about nothing," Louisa's voice echoed to the high ceilings of the hall as she headed up the staircase. Poor thing, trying so hard to hide her concerned feelings. At the same moment Scout raced down with Boss on his heels, whilst Ambrosia navigated the other side, her gnarly, bejewelled fingers clasping the rail with one hand as she used her cane for balance with the other.

"Take care, Scout," Ginger scolded lightly.

"Sorry, Mum. Me and Boss are going outside to play fetch."

"It's 'Boss and I'," Ginger said to his disappearing form.

"What on earth is going on?" Ambrosia said on seeing Ginger standing there. "It's like a circus around here. One can't move from one floor to the other without nearly getting bowled over."

She kept on with her tirade as she carefully negotiated the last step. "Please don't tell me there's been another body. I don't think my nerves could take it."

"No, Grandmother," Ginger said. "Not another body, only a missing one, apparently. Sally's gone off the map."

Ambrosia snorted. "Hardly a reason to call in the cavalry. The lady is probably searching for a bit of peace."

"Basil needs to ask her a few questions about Mr. Doyle. Unfortunately, his death is being considered suspicious, and Basil wants to speak to everyone who knew him." Not only had Sally admitted to knowing Mr. Doyle, Mrs. Beasley's evidence against her was quite damning. *Oh Sally, where are you?*

Ginger hoped her stepmother wasn't in danger, but more than that, she hoped she hadn't run off due to a bout of guilt. What a scandal that would be, if Sally Hartigan was implicated in murder! Poor Ambrosia's nerves would be sure to fail her then.

Basil, with hat in hand and his winter overcoat on, walked towards Ginger.

"Where are you going?" she asked.

"I thought my time would be better spent talking to the next set of suspects."

Ginger felt the nerves in her face twitch at the implication: Louisa and Sally were a set of suspects.

"And who would that be?"

"Ruby Doyle and Alan Lester."

Of course. Family members were always the first to be under suspicion.

"Do you mind if I join you?" Ginger said.

Basil's lips curved into a crooked smile. "I was hoping you would."

9

*I*t had only been a day since Ginger had first visited the Lester siblings, but somehow it felt much longer. She hadn't even had a chance to relay to Basil what had transpired then.

Now that they were travelling through the streets of London with Basil at the wheel of his Austin 7, Ginger had a moment to think. She adjusted her green wool cloche hat, admiring the reflection in the glass.

"I expected awkwardness," Ginger said, "and emotion. One could hardly expect otherwise after the sudden death of someone so close—"

"But?" Basil prompted.

"They were quite guarded, and at one point

spoke out of turn as if they'd forgotten I was in the room."

Basil slowed behind a bright red double decker bus, whose occupants on the open top section looked down at them. "What do you mean?" he asked.

"They mentioned being in danger, and then Mr. Lester tried to make me believe they'd been referring to his travelling to America. He actually claimed he'd never been on a ship because he was a poor swimmer."

"What about his plans to travel to Australia?"

"Exactly."

When they parked in front of the terraced house off Oxford Street, the lights were dim, and Ginger worried that Mr. Lester and his sister weren't at home. How dull if all their suspects continually proved to be difficult to track down. However, she needn't have been concerned, as Mr. Lester himself answered the door after Basil had knocked.

"Mr. Lester," Basil started. "We do apologise for coming uninvited, but it's now a matter of police business that we're here. Would you mind if we came in?"

The question was a polite courtesy, but Ginger knew as well as Mr. Lester that it wasn't a request.

Mr. Lester opened the door and motioned them inside. "Is something the matter?"

"I'm afraid the death of your brother-in-law appears to be suspicious."

Mr. Lester looked truly shocked. "You can't be serious!"

"Unfortunately, I am. We've heard from the pathologist directly."

"But how?"

Mr. Lester's shock seemed to have dulled his manners, Ginger thought, as if he thought the whole interview might be conducted in the hall.

"Do you mind if we sit?" Basil asked.

"Oh, my apologies. Please follow me."

Mr. Lester took them to the same room that Ginger had been in the day before, only this time she and Basil settled on a settee by the fireplace. Ruby Doyle was already seated in one of the chairs, a book resting on her lap.

"Oh, hello," she said as if in a daze.

"Please don't get up," Basil said. "We've only a few questions and then we'll be on our way."

"I see," Mrs. Doyle said. "Has something happened?"

Alan Lester answered before Basil could get the words out. "They say Arnold's death is suspicious."

Mrs. Doyle stilled further, statue-like, until finally she blinked. "What does that mean?"

She and Mr. Lester looked to Basil for an answer.

"Mr. Doyle's cause of death wasn't due to accidental choking. The laboratory reports of the exact cause aren't in, but the preliminary indicators suggest poisoning."

Ruby Doyle became suddenly animated. "That's preposterous! Who would do such a thing?"

Basil moved his hat off his lap and removed a notepad and pencil from the pocket of his overcoat. "That is what I intend to find out, madam."

"What kind of poison was it?" Lester asked.

"That is yet to be determined," Basil said. "The city laboratories are backed up, with workers taking time off over Christmas. I'm hoping for a concrete answer in the next couple of days. Now—"

Ginger carefully watched the siblings whose eyes were working at communicating even if their mouths were not. Ginger couldn't help but feel the two of them were afraid, but of what? Becoming the next victims? Or being caught?

"Mrs. Doyle," Basil began, "how long were you and Mr. Doyle married?"

"Nine years."

"How did you meet?"

"At a party, here in London."

"Did you visit your family here often?"

"No, actually. This is the first time."

"What did Mr. Doyle do for work in New York?"

"Importing and exporting."

Ginger glanced at Basil, then asked, "What kinds of goods did your husband import and export?"

Mrs. Doyle's fingers played nervously with the ruffled collar of her blouse. "Many things. I suppose I don't know exactly. Arnold kept his business ventures to himself."

Many things? Like contraband Canadian whiskey and English rum? Prohibition in the United States was an experiment the whole world was watching. To many foreigners looking on and, Ginger knew, to many nationals as well, the latest amendment to the American constitution was a failure.

"Mr. Lester," Basil said, keeping his eyes on his notes, "did you ever go to New York to visit your sister?"

"Er, no."

"How well did you know Mr. Doyle?"

"Not well. He came here from Dublin before emigrating to America. He and Ruby had a short engagement, you could say."

Ruby Doyle blushed. "I suppose I was swept off my feet. Arnold's bold approach to life felt like a breath of fresh air at the time." Her gaze dropped to her hands now cupped together on her lap. "I longed for adventure, you see."

"Did you and Mr. Doyle get on, Mr. Lester?" Basil asked.

"What do you mean?"

"Did you like your brother-in-law?"

"Arnold Doyle was a bull in a china shop," Mr. Lester said, "a force to be reckoned with. Did I like him? Not particularly. Not many people did." He smiled wanly at his sister. "Sorry, Ruby." Then he turned back to Basil. "I didn't care for Arnold, but I certainly had no reason to kill him."

"What do you do for employment, Mr. Lester?" Basil asked, surprising Alan Lester with the sudden change of subject.

"I work for the Home Office."

"Doesn't that require a certain amount of travel?"

"Yes. I don't own a motorcar so I travel by train. I flew on an aeroplane once." He chuckled dryly. "I don't plan to do it again if I can help it."

"If we were meant to fly, we'd be born with wings," Mrs. Doyle said stiffly. "Arnold used to say that." She revealed a handkerchief that had been twisted in one hand and dabbed at damp eyes.

"I'm not sure what you're expecting to get from us, Chief Inspector," Mr. Lester said. "But, please, out of respect for my sister, I ask that we bring this interview to a close."

"What did you make of that?" Ginger asked quietly, once they were outside and away from Mr. Lester's front door.

"Lester is certainly protective of his sister," Basil said, "which is perfectly understandable."

"His eyes gave him away," Ginger added. "They darkened the moment he calculated that Ruby Doyle would naturally be your prime suspect."

"Doyle was a brute verbally," Basil said. "And did you notice the modesty of Mrs. Doyle's dress? Unlike your evening gown or Felicia's or Louisa's, there wasn't a bit of skin bare on her arms or back."

Of course Ginger had noticed Ruby's long-sleeved floral blouse, fastened snugly at the wrists. Under normal circumstances, Ginger wouldn't have given it a second thought. Every lady had her style, but if Ruby Doyle was intent on hiding evidence that her husband beat her, then her choice of frock was perfect.

Ginger's thoughts went to Sally, who, at the moment, was suspect number two. Her interference in the kitchen on the day of the murder and her strange behaviour since didn't bode well. Ginger's stomach clenched.

She hovered while Basil approached Constable Braxton on the pavement.

"Any word on Doyle's background check?" Basil asked.

"Yes, sir. Apparently, Arnold Doyle had dealings with an American mob called The White Hand Gang. I'm not sure how that could be connected to the goings on here."

Ginger and Basil glanced at each other. That was the very gang that had been reported in the news.

"What kind of dealings?" Basil said.

"The telegrams that have reached us from the police in New York stated that Mr. Doyle was on the outside of the gang. Got himself into a disagreement with Richard Lonergan, and came out on the losing side."

"The same Richard Lonergan who was killed at a Brooklyn speakeasy?"

"Yes, sir."

The crisp, damp mist prompted them to lengthen their strides to get to the vehicle. Basil said something to Constable Braxton then slid into the driver's seat of his Austin and slammed the door against the rain. The window was too fogged up to see through and they madly wiped the windscreen clear with their gloves.

"Is that why he came to London?" Ginger asked now safely inside the vehicle, her umbrella shaken out and collapsed. "But why arrange to come to Hartigan House?" she added. "Why single me out when I never knew him from Adam?"

"Good question," Basil said.

Ginger mused. "There must've been someone in attendance at the Christmas dinner who had something he needed, who could help him somehow."

Basil caught her eye as he drove. "Didn't he want to talk to you?"

"Yes. But it remains a mystery how he thought I might have been able to help. I don't even know what his perceived problem was. He died before he could get to it."

"My guess is money. A bloke like that wouldn't think twice before swindling a wealthy lady."

Ginger snorted. "He certainly didn't know me well, if he thought that would work."

Basil grinned. "Indeed." The windscreen had fogged up again and he wiped it with his glove.

"I'm going to call at Mr. and Mrs. Davenport's house. Would you like me to drop you off at home first? I know it's been a long day already."

"Actually," Ginger said nonchalantly, "I've already been to see them."

"You have?" Basil shifted gears as he sped along the main road. Ginger wondered how her husband managed in the soupy fog that had settled into the narrow streets while they had been inside Mr. Lester's house.

"I felt it my duty to check on them," Ginger explained. "After the shock. Especially Mrs. Davenport. She's so frightfully frail."

"You've a good heart, Lady Gold," Basil said with a teasing smile. "And though I don't doubt the altruistic nature of your visit, I'm betting you were slipping in a bit of sleuthing as well."

"One can do both without marring one's conscience."

"Indeed," Basil agreed. "And what did you learn?"

Ginger turned her face towards the window, regretting now that she'd brought the subject up. But no, she was determined not to keep things from Basil, especially if she wanted them to continue to success-fully work together.

"I saw Sally leaving when I arrived. She didn't see me."

Basil glanced over with widened eyes. "Did you know that she was acquainted with them?"

"No, but Sally lived here for a while before she married my father. They met at a London club, I'm told. So, she could know people without me being aware of it."

"One would be forgiven for not assuming so," Basil said. "They didn't act like they knew each other at the dinner."

"And when I asked Mr. Davenport if he knew Sally, he lied."

"He lied?"

"At least he meant to mislead me. I asked him if he'd had a visitor before I arrived and he looked me straight in the eye and said no."

Basil rubbed his chin, now showing signs of a shadow. "How bewildering."

A POLICE VEHICLE was already sitting in front of the Davenports' house, and Ginger assumed this was the instruction Basil had given to Constable Braxton.

The young officer exited the motorcar when he saw them arrive.

"As far as I can tell," Constable Braxton said, "they're at home, sir."

Once again, Ginger was grateful for her umbrella and managed to stay relatively dry as they walked to the front door. The butler answered the door after Basil rang the bell.

"I'm Chief Inspector Basil Reed. Please let Mr. and Mrs. Davenport know that I'd like to see them. This is police business and I'm here with Constable Braxton and my consultant, Lady Gold."

Ginger always found it rather thrilling when Basil introduced her as Lady Gold, her former title and the alias she used as an investigator. It conveniently distanced her during formal interviews from being Basil's wife, which made her feel like an interloper.

It was a bit odd, though, in light of the fact that the Davenports were family friends of Ruby Doyle and Alan Lester, but it gave a sense of seriousness that was warranted by the situation.

When the butler led them to the sitting room, Mr. Davenport was there alone.

"Please forgive Mrs. Davenport. She is unwell and remains in her bed."

"I hope it's not serious," Ginger stated. She rather liked Mrs. Davenport and felt deep empathy for her as the lady struggled to cope with her losses. Not everyone was able to find a new sense of normality after the destruction wrought by the war.

"The doctor has seen her," was Mr. Davenport's answer. The man seemed to have aged overnight—his grey hair unoiled and the stoop in his shoulders more severe. "Please be seated."

Mr. Davenport settled heavily into a highbacked leather armchair to the side of an active flame in the fireplace, while Basil and Ginger took the settee. Constable Braxton remained at the ready by the door.

"I won't offer you drinks, as it's quite obvious this isn't a social call," Mr. Davenport said wearily. He reached for his pipe and a match, which lay on the small occasional table to his right. The bowl of the pipe glowed red as he lit the tobacco, inhaled, and then released a stream of smoke into the air.

"I'm afraid not," Basil said. "Arnold Doyle's death is considered suspicious. We're obligated to interview everyone who was acquainted with Mr. Doyle and who was present at the Christmas dinner."

"I'll make this easy for you then," Mr. Davenport

said, after another tobacco-scented puff. "I'm ready to confess."

Ginger and Basil shot each other a sideways glance before staring back at the older gentleman.

"You're confessing to the murder of Mr. Arnold Doyle?" Basil asked.

Mr. Davenport nodded slowly. "Yes."

"But why?" Ginger asked. For the life of her, she couldn't think of a motive. What connection did Mr. Davenport have with Arnold Doyle to merit such an extreme action?

"I was being blackmailed."

"By whom?" Basil asked.

"It hardly matters, does it?" Mr. Davenport said. "The man's dead and I killed him."

"How did you kill him?" Basil asked.

"Poison, obviously."

Ginger objected, "But Mrs. Gupta was sitting between you and Mr. Doyle. How did you administer it without interfering with her?"

Mr. Davenport shifted, clearly uncomfortable under the weight of the interrogation. "Like I said, what does it matter? I did it. Now, should I come to the station to make my statement?"

Ginger looked at Basil, seeing the doubt that flashed behind her husband's eyes. Mr. Davenport was a terrible liar, but rather perceptive. As if he had had second thoughts, he offered an explanation.

"I'll tell you everything I know, but please keep in mind that Mrs. Davenport knew nothing about this. Nothing at all."

Some men might say that to protect their wives, but Ginger had a strong feeling Mr. Davenport was telling the truth about this.

He continued, "I had a vial of cyanide. I simply poured it into his drink when no one was watching."

They had mingled for a while over drinks in the drawing room, before the meal progressed. Then again, it had taken at least an hour and a half for them to get through the meal and into dessert. Ginger was fairly certain cyanide poisoning didn't take that long to become effective.

Basil turned and spoke over his shoulder. "Constable Braxton. Please arrest Mr. Davenport on the suspicion of murder of Mr. Arnold Doyle."

10

The shock of Mr. Davenport's confession had eclipsed the worry Ginger felt over Sally's disappearance, and she had to admit she'd quite forgotten about her stepmother's plight. Pippins, who had greeted her and Basil at the back entrance of Hartigan House, was quick to give her good news.

"Mrs. Hartigan is here, and unharmed," he said as he took their coats and Basil's hat.

"Oh, thank goodness," Ginger said. "Where is she?"

"I believe she and Miss Hartigan are in the library, madam."

Ginger and Basil were in the corridor when they

were nearly bowled over by an exuberant Scout and Boss.

"Whoa," Basil said. "Slow down, young man."

Boss had detoured into the dining room and Ginger caught up with both Scout and her pet there.

"You shouldn't run about the house," Ginger said, scolding mildly. "It wouldn't do if you knocked someone over." An unpleasant image of Ambrosia losing her balance came to mind.

Scout lowered his chin. "Yes, Mum."

"You should take your games outside."

"But it's raining."

Ginger worked her lips. Her son had a point.

Scout's eyes brightened with an idea.

"Could we play in the attic? There's loads of room up there and I promise to stay away from the bedrooms."

The attic was where the live-in members of the staff slept, though there were only three at the moment. Pippins and Clement were in one end and Mrs. Beasley in the other. Scout had once had a bedroom up there.

"I suppose that would be a good alternative," Ginger said. "But do be sure to respect the private property of others."

"Yes, Mum."

Scout called Boss who seemed quite taken with one of the chairs around the table, sniffing at the legs and even licking them.

"Boss?" Ginger said with alarm. "What are you doing?"

The dog stared up with wide, innocent eyes, then chased after Scout, who'd beckoned him to follow.

Ginger wrinkled her brow. "How odd."

She found Basil upstairs with a sombre-looking Sally Hartigan, but it appeared they had yet to discuss anything important. Sally rolled her eyes when she saw Ginger. "I hear I've caused an uproar just because I didn't register with the front desk when I left."

It was a snide allusion to Sally complaining that she felt like a hotel guest rather than family.

Ginger didn't bother to insult her stepmother's intelligence by pretending their concern wasn't motivated by something other than her well-being. "Louisa," Ginger said, "if you wouldn't mind giving us a moment."

Louisa stared back, looking entirely put out. "Why should I? I'd like to know what my own mother's been up to."

In a rare instant of maternal authority, Sally refused to let Louisa have her way. "Louisa, go."

Sniffing loudly so that no one could misinterpret her affront, Louisa tightened her fists and marched out of the room, taking a good amount of oxygen with her, Ginger thought. She inhaled deeply then took Louisa's empty chair.

"Sally," Ginger began, "you should know that your American acquaintance Mr. Doyle's death wasn't accidental. Mr. Davenport has confessed to his murder."

Sally's head jerked up and her jaw dropped open. "What? No."

"I'm afraid it's true," Basil said.

"He *confessed*? What did he say exactly?"

Ginger hadn't been sure what kind of reaction Sally would have to the news, but it wasn't this. Sally seemed sincerely distressed, more so than one would expect from someone who'd barely known the other.

But then again, Ginger had seen her stepmother sneak out of the Davenport residence.

"Mr. Davenport confessed to adding cyanide to Mr. Doyle's drink before dinner," Basil said.

Sally's wide-eyed gaze moved from Basil to Ginger. "But—that's impossible."

Ginger stared back in question. "Why is that?"

"Because I still have the vial! It was I who was meant to kill Arnold Doyle. But he died before I had a chance!"

"Sally!" Ginger shook her head in confusion. "What are you going on about?"

"I have the poison. Bertram Davenport couldn't have done it. Besides, why would he?"

"Mr. Davenport claims he was being black-mailed," Ginger said. "Why would *you*?"

"Because *I* was the one being blackmailed. Mr. Davenport was simply trying to help me out of a terrible situation." Her eyes were imploring. "I know it's a horrible thing, to admit to premeditated murder, but I swear to you, I didn't go through with it. Arnold died before I had a chance."

"If that's true," Basil said, "then Mr. Davenport is innocent as well. Why would he lie on your behalf, Mrs. Hartigan?"

"Because Mr. Davenport is my great-uncle."

Ginger's jaw dropped. "How could I not know that?"

"You don't know everything about me, Ginger. My roots are in England. Though most of my family emigrated to America years ago, I still have a family line on my mother's side here. Bertram is my mother's uncle. It's why I was in London when I met your father. I was visiting family."

"Who was blackmailing you, Mrs. Hartigan?" Basil asked.

Sally's eyes grew glossy with tears. "Richard Lonergan."

Ginger couldn't help but gape at the pronouncement. "The leader of The White Hand Gang? Whatever for?"

"Oh, Ginger! He said if I did away with Mr. Doyle, he'd preserve George's reputation."

That could explain why Sally had been lurking about the kitchen. She was looking for ways to poison Arnold Doyle, without killing everyone else.

"Father's reputation?" Ginger stated. Her father had passed away five and a half years ago. "How was he possibly mixed up in this?"

Sally stared at Ginger, her cat-like eyes beseeching. "I suppose I have to come clean. It was *I* who made a sour investment with Mr. Doyle. Mr. Lonergan—we become acquainted recently through mutual social contacts—bailed me out, but I had to do him a favour in return. It's a sordid affair, and I'm quite ashamed. I just want it to all go away." She smiled wanly. "Maybe now, with both Mr. Doyle and Mr. Lonergan dead, it will."

Sally produced a handkerchief and dabbed at tears that had formed in the corners of her eyes. "I'm sorry, I'm just so relieved. It's the best kind of serendipity. I'm finally free of the man and I didn't have to commit a crime in the end to do it."

Ginger sank in her chair. What a bizarre twist of fate.

Ginger nibbled a long nail. Sally's news wasn't all that remarkable, except that she had kept her acquaintance with Arnold Doyle secret even though they had all sat around the table together.

"That accounts for your surprise arrival," Ginger said. "You were following Mr. Doyle."

Sally lifted a shoulder, then stared at the window. "I couldn't believe my good fortune when I heard he was coming to see you. I bet he wanted to drag you into one of his horrendous schemes. He was always after your father to invest in some shenanigan or another."

Ginger couldn't help but think that her stepmother had dodged a very large bullet. But, if Mr. Davenport and Sally hadn't killed Arnold Doyle, then who had?

11

The news Ginger and Basil received the next morning confirmed one thing and opened a Pandora's Box concerning another.

"Dr. Gupta is sure?" Ginger asked.

Basil shrugged and lifted his palms. "He definitely said that there was no poison in Arnold Doyle's system."

"Then, are we back to accidental death?"

Basil shook his head. "Dr. Gupta said Doyle died of a food reaction. The laboratory results were clear that the culprit was peanuts."

Ginger inhaled as understanding dawned. "Mr. Doyle clearly stated he didn't like nuts, peanuts in particular. Mrs. Doyle said they made him cough."

"Perhaps they were underplaying the effects."

"I knew someone in Boston who got deathly ill from eating peanut butter," Ginger stated. Peanuts were common in America, but rather difficult to find in England, unless they were specially imported. Ginger felt a sense of relief. She, herself, reviewed the receipts that came through the kitchen and was confident that an order or purchase of peanuts had never been made.

Ginger continued, "Who would've known about the peanut reaction, and how could they have put peanuts in Mr. Doyle's meal without anyone noticing?"

"Sleight of hand?" Basil suggested.

Ginger's mind went back to Boss' odd behaviour from the day before. "Peanut oil," she said. "Yesterday I caught Boss licking one of the chairs in the dining room. It makes sense now. He smelt peanut oil residue."

"Was it Ruby Doyle's chair?" Basil asked.

Ginger held Basil's gaze. "No. It was Alan Lester's."

"We have to get that chair to Scotland Yard before anyone else touches it. I'll call the Yard now and get someone to pick Alan Lester up and take him to the station for questioning."

Ginger felt stunned by the sudden revelation.

Was Alan Lester really their man? Had he killed his brother-in-law?

He certainly had motive and opportunity, but what of means? How did he get the peanut oil onto Arnold Doyle's plate of food?

It couldn't have been in the pudding, since that had been made several weeks before. But what about the brandy butter? Mr. Lester had added the brandy butter to his piece of pudding before pushing it away. No one would've noticed if a little peanut oil had been added.

Mr. Lester knew his brother-in-law's penchant for overindulging. It was a risk—a worm on the line—but Arnold Doyle took the bait, and died for it.

It was rather ingenious, Ginger had to admit. The days they had spent trying to put the pieces together, especially over the festive season, would have given Alan Lester the time he needed to put his next step into action. Ginger wouldn't be surprised if Mr. Lester was, at that very moment, attempting to flee the country.

GINGER INTENDED to drop in to Feathers & Flair, but the parking spot most readily available was around the corner near her Lady Gold Investigations office, so she decided to call in there first. A short step down into a shallow concrete recess led to the front door. Ginger held on to the rail, damp with rain, with one hand and Boss, tucked under her arm, with the other. At the landing, she fished out her keys from her handbag, but found the door unlocked. Ginger's heart skipped a beat. Had someone broken in?

She held a finger to her lips, a sign for Boss to stay quiet, and opened the door silently—with practice one could open it without knocking the bell—then padded softly through the small waiting room and into the larger office area.

Felicia looked up from her seat at her desk, hands hovering over the keys of her black typewriter.

"Ginger! I didn't expect you."

"Nor I you." Ginger released the breath she'd been holding as she set Boss onto the hard wooden floor and instructed him to go to the wicker dog bed. She removed her gloves as she strolled to her desk. "What are you doing here?"

Felicia stared back with pinched lips, and Ginger had a feeling she knew what was going on.

"Louisa, is it?"

Felicia let out a puff of air. "I know she's your half-sister—you have blood between you, we don't.

And I do adore her, but she's simply exhausting to be around all the time. I had to sneak off just to hear myself think."

The pot was indeed busy calling the kettle black.

"Besides," Felicia continued, "I had a great idea for my novel."

Felicia's latest passion was mystery novel writing. To everyone's amazement, she had actually found a publisher, though she'd had to use the masculine-sounding name of Frank Gold to garner initial attention.

Felicia turned the question back on Ginger. "What are you doing here?"

"Besides the fact that this is my place of business, I was in the area, you could say. I'm going to Feathers & Flair next to try on my gown for New Year's Eve."

"I've got to get over there myself today for a slight alteration," Felicia said with delight. "Hemlines, as you know, are rising, and I want to bare every inch of leg I can legally get away with!" Felicia threw her legs out from under her desk and scissored them in demonstration. Ginger couldn't keep from grinning. Felicia was far more like Louisa than her former sister-in-law would like to admit.

"Any business-related news?" Ginger asked. A stack of letters sat on her desk and she fished through them. "Most of these are bills. You can see to them getting paid, can't you?"

Felicia wrinkled her nose at the idea of doing actual work for her pay and sighed, agreeing, "If I must."

The telephone rang and Felicia and Ginger stared each other down until Felicia relented and answered.

"Good afternoon, Lady Gold Investigations. Yes, operator, I'll wait." Felicia put a hand over the mouthpiece. "It's Scotland Yard."

Ginger reached out her arm and Felicia smirked as she handed over the heavy receiver.

"Hello, Basil," she said warmly. She never tired of hearing her husband's voice, but she knew this wasn't a social call, not if it was coming from the Yard.

"Ginger, I've just got word from my men who were following Alan Lester. He's gone to Euston Station. I believe he's going to try to flee the country."

"Oh mercy. Is Ruby with him?"

"The officer never mentioned her, but if his sister is part of the getaway plan, I may need your help with her."

"Of course. I'll meet you there."

. . .

GINGER'S LATE HUSBAND, Daniel, Lord Gold, had given Ginger a palm-sized silver Remington Derringer pistol as a gift before he headed back to England from Boston to join the British Army. She rarely used it, of course, but it brought her a sense of comfort knowing it was tucked away nicely in her handbag.

Ginger drove rapidly through Fitzrovia and past University College, hitting a pothole and splashing a man walking his dog. He held up a fist in protest.

"Whoa," Felicia cried, theatrically placing a gloved hand on her downturned hat, decorated liber-ally with colourful feathers. "I'd like to get there in one piece, if you don't mind."

She was completely overdoing her angst, Ginger thought.

"Very funny, Felicia. Time is rather of the essence, but if you'd prefer I drop you off so you can wave down a taxicab or take the underground, I'd be happy to oblige."

Ginger caught Felicia rolling her eyes, but the girl wisely kept her pouty mouth shut. They were nearly at the station anyway.

The big Roman pillars of the Euston Arch came

into view and Ginger parked the Crossley on Drummond Street. She and Felicia, with Boss scampering behind, joined the crowds that entered the station through the stone pillars.

Alongside her Remington, Ginger also carried a pair of opera glasses. Perfect for bird watching or enjoying the Ascot races, today Ginger used them to scan the sea of faces in the great hall, searching for anyone who looked familiar. Not an easy task, considering most of the men wore overcoats in shades of brown or grey and similar-coloured trilby or bowler hats on their heads.

The blue police uniforms were a welcome contrast in the mix and soon Ginger found an officer of the law, stretching on his toes, peering through the crowd. Ginger zoomed in on his face and muttered aloud, "Constable Braxton."

"Constable Braxton?" Felicia said, straining her long neck in an effort to see. "Where?"

"By the rear door going to the platforms."

Felicia started in that direction, but Ginger grabbed her arm. "Wait. We mustn't get in the way of law enforcement."

"Yes, you're right. What should we do then?"

"Act normally. Let's go and buy a platform ticket."

Ginger scooped Boss into her arms as they stood in the queue, and when they got to the clerk who stood at a counter on the other side of an opened glass window, Ginger stated her order. While the transaction was completed, she asked, "Have you seen a man in his early thirties with dark hair? He has one blue and one brown eye. He might've been with a lady."

The clerk's eyebrows jumped. "Oh, I did see such a fellow. 'Ard to know which eye to look at. Bought tickets for 'isself and 'is wife, though she wasn't with 'im at the time."

"To Liverpool?"

"Yes, madam."

"Which platform?"

"Three, madam."

"Thank you," Ginger said. She pocketed the tickets.

"Wife?" Felicia remarked.

"A ruse, I suspect." Alan Lester knew the police would be looking for a brother and sister together. Ginger linked her arm with Felicia's, the only sure way not to lose her in the masses. They passed through the platform barrier where passengers waited under the wrought-iron roof.

Suddenly, they were jostled about by the people

around them, and Ginger nearly got an elbow to the ribs.

Someone shouted, "Stop, police!"

Ginger's pulse kept rising. She knew the voice. She looked about for Basil's form and found him, pushing his way through the crowd. A man Ginger could only assume was Alan Lester raced away ahead, roughly pushing passengers out of his way, and turned down Platform 3, where the Liverpool train stood, steam hissing from its engine.

Ginger followed through the tunnel that formed after Basil, keeping her eyes on his head, the shape of which she knew so well. Felicia fell behind, with a whimper.

Constable Braxton raced ahead, darting through the crowd, many of whom had stopped in their tracks, gawking.

Basil's voice reached Ginger again, as he shouted for Mr. Lester to stop, though his efforts were proving to be in vain.

Ginger released Boss, letting him run. "Find Constable Braxton! And be careful!"

If only there were a way to catch up with Alan Lester, Ginger thought, but the crowds and her heels worked against her. Passengers were boarding the train, which, according to the large round clock hanging overhead, was about to leave in two minutes.

Ginger darted a glance through the windows of the train. The adjacent track was empty; a train had pulled out not five minutes earlier. The empty platform! Ginger turned around, pushing back against the flow of the crowd, and raced towards the head of the track.

"Ginger!" Felicia shouted as Ginger ran past the engine. "Where are you going?"

Ginger just flapped her hand in passing as she turned the corner to the next platform. No time to explain! She raced along the empty platform, trying to peer through the train windows, attempting to catch a glance of what was happening on Platform 3. There! That was Lester, still pushing through the crowds! Ginger put on a renewed burst of speed, and another quick glance told her she had outpaced him.

She stopped and squatted down at the edge of the platform. Shoes on or off? No, even though the heels were a hindrance, the rough stone of the track would be impossible to move on in bare feet. She jumped down onto the empty tracks, picked her way across the rails, then reached up as far as she could, just barely able to reach the door handle of the nearest carriage. She swung herself up onto the metal grid of the step, wincing as she heard the ripping sound of her skirt seam giving way, and pulled open the door. Two steps through the carriage to the other side, and there, a few yards beyond her on the platform, were Lester and Constable Braxton, who had just caught up with his quarry.

The officer lifted his truncheon, but it was quite obvious who'd been trained by the British military and who had not, and in an instant, Constable Braxton was caught in a headlock and at Mr. Lester's mercy.

Mr. Lester shouted at Basil who was only a few steps away, "Stand back or I'll break his neck!"

Basil lifted his arms in the air. "Easy, old chap," he said. "We don't want to hurt you."

Alan Lester's eyes darted rapidly side to side, as if he was trying to calculate a way out. Beads of sweat formed on his forehead and he tightened his hold on the constable. He snorted, then shouted, "Then get out of my way!"

"We can't do that, now," Basil soothed. "You know that. Just come quietly, and I'll make sure the judge knows you cooperated."

"No judge cares a fig about me! I have to look after myself."

"What about Ruby?"

Both Basil and Alan Lester jerked at the sound of Ginger's voice. She'd climbed down onto the platform without being noticed and had her fingers wrapped around the Remington, nicely nestled away in her coat pocket.

"Why did you do it?" Basil asked.

Mr. Lester narrowed his eyes at Basil, but actually relaxed his hold on Constable Braxton. The poor officer gulped a breath. Mr. Lester offered his explanation. "The man was a liar, a thief, and a brute. He hit my sister and tried to keep her from her family. We hadn't seen her since they got married nine years ago. When I heard he was actually bringing her back to England, I knew I had to take my chance. I did it for Ruby."

"As a family member, you were aware of your brother-in-law's reaction to peanuts?"

"Yes. It wasn't well known. I'd brought back a jar of peanut butter from my last visit. I travelled all the way to New York to see my sister and Doyle barely gave us a minute to be alone together. He stole Ruby from me. Somehow she'd got a chance to send me a letter without Doyle intercepting her efforts, letting me know they were coming. I decided there and then I would do whatever it took to free my sister."

"So you added a bit of peanut oil to your portion of brandy butter," Ginger said.

"The hand is quicker than the eye," Mr. Lester said. "You couldn't tell the difference with brandy butter already oily." He scowled. "You were supposed to think Doyle had choked."

It would've worked, Ginger thought, if not for modern forensic science coming into play. And Boss' keen sense of smell.

Speaking of Boss, where had he gone? Ginger glanced about for her pet while carefully keeping her target in sight.

Basil's questioning kept Alan Lester focused on him, and away from where Ginger was positioned. She slipped behind the man, unnoticed by him.

"It's over, Mr. Lester," Ginger said as she pressed the nose of her pistol against his back. "Let the constable go."

"Just shoot me!" Mr. Lester said. His hold on Constable Braxton tightened and the officer squirmed, making choking sounds.

Ginger applied more pressure between the man's shoulder blades. "Let him go."

"Shoot me!"

"I can't do that, Mr. Lester, without the possibility of hurting Constable Braxton too."

Sweat dripped from Mr. Lester's temple. He was a wild man in a jungle, with the beasts pressing in and no flaming torch to hold them back.

Suddenly Boss latched on to the hem of Mr. Lester's coat, and with a determined growl, began to tug, pulling the man off balance just enough for Constable Braxton to break loose from the chokehold.

Basil reached them, his handcuffs ready. "Mr. Alan Lester," he said, "you're under arrest for the murder of Arnold Doyle."

12

The mood at Hartigan House had shifted remarkably by the time New Year's Eve arrived, the dreadful affair of a week ago nearly forgotten. Everyone was preparing, in their own way, to bring in a brand-new year.

Ginger sat before her dressing table mirror putting on the finishing touches of her make-up. Smoky eyeshadow blended with blue brushed towards thinly plucked and arched brows. Several coats of mascara thickened her dark lashes, framing bright green eyes. An evening like this merited the dark red lipstick she applied, producing the desired bow shape made famous by the American film star Clara Bow.

Boss, ever watchful, whimpered his appreciation.

"I'm sorry you can't come tonight," Ginger said to his reflection in her mirror. "Dreadfully unfair, I know, but no dogs are allowed at the ball. I'll make sure Scout gives you an extra treat." Ginger scrubbed her pet behind his pointy ears and kissed his head. "Goodness knows you deserve it."

Ginger's old journal caught her eye. Perhaps it was the whimsy that comes with the approach of a new year—all the hopes and dreams ignited that will either rise or fall over the course of the next twelve months—or perhaps it was the nature of the festive season to recall days of old. She was reminded of the line spoken by the Ghost of Christmas Past to Ebenezer Scrooge, "These are but shadows of things that have been".

She began reading about the Christmas from so long ago.

Father and I helped in the kitchen while Sally and Louisa "helped" serve coffee and cut cake after the meal was over. Mostly they just hovered, grimacing with disapproval.

Reading about her father, so very much alive, made Ginger's heart ache. Her mother had died shortly after Ginger's birth, and for most of her life her father had been her whole world. Ginger would always miss him.

The guests weren't eager to return to the cold and many of them lingered about the fire as they sipped hot coffee. I recognised the lady from the street I'd seen on the ride over. Up close she looked frail, with bony fingers and dark circles around her eyes. Even though the blaze in the hearth and the numerous bodies had warmed up the room, she'd never taken her winter coat off. I was alarmed to find her shivering and it became clear to me that her coat was threadbare and could in no way ward off the biting Boston wind and cold.

Immediately I went to the back room where the staff kept their things, retrieved my fur-trimmed coat, and hurried back to the hall. At first I couldn't spot the woman, and my heart sank, but then a larger figure moved aside and she was there.

I approached her and introduced myself.

"Hello, I'm Miss Ginger Hartigan."

"Ma'am. My name's Mrs. Gladys Parker."

"Pleased to meet you, Mrs. Parker. I hope I'm not being too forward, but I wondered if you'd like this?"

I held up my coat.

Mrs. Parker stared back with bewilderment. "What'cha mean?"

"It's a Christmas present. For you," I added.

Mrs. Parker eyed my jacket with longing. I wondered when the last time was that she'd felt truly warm.

"Please, try it on," I coaxed. Without removing her own outer wear, Mrs. Parker extended a thin arm, but before she could shrug the coat on, Sally rudely interrupted.

"Ginger Hartigan! What on earth are you doing?"

I stared at my stepmother with steely reserve. "I'm going to give this lady my coat."

"Well, stop it this instant. It's brand new from Filenes!"

I answered defiantly, "I'll just get another one."

"She's right," Mrs. Parker said as she pushed the coat my way. "I couldn't accept your charity."

Sally scoffed. "Of course you could. Isn't that the way of your type? Living on the handouts of others."

It was my turn to protest. "Sally!"

"Well, it's true," Sally said, unruffled. "You can't just give every impoverished person the coat off your back."

"I'm not giving it to everyone. I'm giving it to Mrs. Parker." I pressed the coat back into Gladys Parker's arms.

Sally's stubbornness had no bounds. "She's just going to turn around and sell it."

I could be just as obstinate. "It's now hers to do with as she pleases."

"This is ridiculous. I'm telling your father this instant." Sally strode across the hall in her pompous style and I watched as she spoke rapidly with my father, her eyes blazing with indignation.

Mrs. Parker's dark eyes studied me with admiration. "I'da got slapped upside my head if I'd ever spoke to my ma like that, God bless her soul."

"Thankfully, that lady's not my mother."

Mrs. Parker held my jacket out to me. "You should take this back."

"No," I insisted. "I've given it to you. It's yours to enjoy however you wish."

"I can't thank you enough, miss. I promise to do good to someone hurting more than me, as soon as the opportunity arises, miss." I smiled as I watched her put the coat on and fiddle with the large buttons.

"It's so fancy!" she proclaimed with a childlike glee. For the first time that evening I saw her smile. She was wise enough to leave before Sally came back with my father in tow. I let out a defeated sigh at the sight of them strolling slowly toward me.

"Ginger," my father began, "am I to understand you've given away your new winter coat?"

"Yes, Father."

"Even though it's new from Filenes?"

"Yes, Father."

"And that the recipient might sell it for food or lodging and not even wear it at all?"

"Yes, Father."

His face broke into a grand smile. "Oh, Ginger, my love. I'm so proud of you."

"George!" Sally sputtered, obviously expecting a different response. "What is she supposed to wear home?"

"I believe there's an extra horse blanket in the carriage."

Sally's eyelashes fluttered in disbelief. "You're really going to let your daughter wear a horse blanket? In public?"

"Of course not. She will have my coat and I will wear the horse blanket."

"George, you can be so infuriating!"

"Perhaps," Father said genially. "Our good Saviour had even less on the night he was born. I will survive it."

My heart burst with love for my father in that moment. I threw myself into his arms and hugged him tightly. I really couldn't imagine life without him.

Oh, Father, Ginger thought as she wiped a stray

tear. Christmas was such a beautiful time of year, but it could also be heart-wrenching.

She returned the journal to the drawer and closed it just as Basil entered, wearing smart evening wear with a crisp white shirt and black satin top hat. Ginger was certain she'd be the envy of all the ladies at the ball.

Basil seemed equally enamoured with Ginger's ivory satin and lace gown with an abundance of sequins that sparkled in the light. On her red bob she wore a glittering tiara that had a thin strand of exquisite jewels that rested delicately across her forehead.

"You are ravishingly beautiful, love." He ran a finger tenderly along her cheek. "I daresay I'll have to be on my guard tonight or some rogue scallywag will attempt to steal you away."

Ginger laughed as she linked her arm with his. "Let's go to the Ritz."

If you enjoyed reading *Murder by Plum Pudding* please help others enjoy it too.

Recommend it: Help others find the book

by recommending it to friends, readers' groups, discussion boards and by **suggesting it to your local library.**

Review it: Please tell other readers why you liked this book by reviewing it **at leestrauss-books.com**

* No spoilers please *

MURDER ON FLEET STREET
The Ginger Gold Mysteries Book # 12

Murder's a Deadly Secret

Mrs. Ginger Reed—the former Lady Gold—thought her past was dead and buried, but when the mysterious death of a British Secret Service agent threatens to expose her own Great War secrets, she faced with an unimaginable dilemma: break her legal vow to the Official Secrets Act or join the agency again, something she's loathed to do.

Because once they own your soul, there's no getting it back.

Shop at leestraussbooks.com

WANT to start from the beginning? Don't miss the first book of this acclaimed series ~ MURDER ON THE SS. ROSA

Murder's a pain in the bow!

It's 1923 and bright young thing Ginger Gold makes a cross-Atlantic journey from Boston to London, England. When the ship's captain is found dead in a most intriguing fashion, Ginger is only too happy to lend her assistance to the handsome Chief Inspector Basil Reed.

This fun, jazz-age whodunit has readers saying "Lady Gold is a charming heroine" and "can't stop reading!"

Murder on the SS Rosa will have you laughing, crying, and guessing until the last page.

Get started and download the first book in this binge-worthy series today. Shop at leestraussbooks.com

MORE FROM LEE STRAUSS

Shop at leestraussbooks.com

GINGER GOLD MYSTERY SERIES (cozy 1920s historical)

Cozy. Charming. Filled with Bright Young Things. This Jazz Age murder mystery will entertain and delight you with its 1920s flair and pizzazz!

Murder on the SS Rosa

Murder at Hartigan House

Murder at Bray Manor

Murder at Feathers & Flair

Murder at the Mortuary

Murder at Kensington Gardens

Murder at St. George's Church

The Wedding of Ginger & Basil

Murder Aboard the Flying Scotsman

Murder at the Boat Club

Murder on Eaton Square

Murder by Plum Pudding

Murder on Fleet Street

Murder at Brighton Beach

Murder in Hyde Park

Murder at the Royal Albert Hall

Murder in Belgravia

Murder on Mallowan Court

Murder at the Savoy

Murder at the Circus

Murder in France

Murder at Yuletide

Murder at Madame Tussauds

Murder at St. Paul's Cathedral

LADY GOLD INVESTIGATES (Ginger Gold companion short stories)

Volume 1

Volume 2

Volume 3

Volume 4

Volume 5

HIGGINS & HAWKE MYSTERY SERIES (cozy 1930s historical)

The 1930s meets Rizzoli & Isles in this friendship depression era cozy mystery series.

Death at the Tavern

Death on the Tower

Death on Hanover

Death by Dancing

Death on Tremont Street

THE ROSA REED MYSTERIES

(1950s cozy historical)

Murder at High Tide

Murder on the Boardwalk

Murder at the Bomb Shelter

Murder on Location

Murder and Rock 'n Roll

Murder at the Races

Murder at the Dude Ranch

Murder in London

Murder at the Fiesta

Murder at the Weddings

A NURSERY RHYME MYSTERY SERIES (mystery/sci fi)

Marlow finds himself teamed up with intelligent and savvy Sage Farrell, a girl so far out of his league he feels blinded in her presence - literally - damned glasses! Together they work to find the identity of @gingerbreadman. Can they stop the killer before he strikes again?

Gingerbread Man

Life Is but a Dream

Hickory Dickory Dock

Twinkle Little Star

LIGHT & LOVE (sweet romance)

Set in the dazzling charm of Europe, follow Katja, Gabriella, Eva, Anna and Belle as they find strength, hope and love.

Love Song

Your Love is Sweet

In Light of Us

Lying in Starlight

PLAYING WITH MATCHES (WW2 history/romance)

A sobering but hopeful journey about how one young German boy copes with the war and propaganda. Based on true events.

A Piece of Blue String (companion short story)

THE CLOCKWISE COLLECTION (YA time travel romance)

Casey Donovan has issues: hair, height and uncontrollable trips to the 19th century! And now this ~ she's accidentally taken Nate Mackenzie, the cutest boy in the school, back in time. Awkward.

Clockwise

Clockwiser

Like Clockwork

Counter Clockwise

Clockwork Crazy

Clocked (companion novella)

<u>Standalones</u>

Seaweed

Love, Tink

ABOUT THE AUTHOR

Lee Strauss is a USA TODAY bestselling author of The Ginger Gold Mysteries series, The Higgins & Hawke Mystery series, The Rosa Reed Mystery series (cozy historical mysteries), A Nursery Rhyme Mystery series (mystery suspense), The Perception series (young adult dystopian), The Light & Love series (sweet romance), The Clockwise Collection (YA time travel romance), and young adult historical fiction with over a million books read. She has translated titles and a growing audio library.

When Lee's not writing or reading she likes to cycle, hike, and stare at the ocean. She loves to drink caffè lattes and red wines in exotic places, and eat dark chocolate anywhere.

For more info on books by Lee Strauss and her social media links, visit leestraussbooks.com. To make sure you don't miss the next new release, be sure to sign up for her newsletter!

Did you know you can follow your favourite authors on Bookbub? If you subscribe to Bookbub — (and if you don't, why don't you? - They'll send you daily emails alerting you to sales and new releases on just the kind of books you like to read!) — follow me to make sure you don't miss the next Ginger Gold Mystery!

www.leestraussbooks.com
leestraussbooks@gmail.com
facebook.com/AuthorLeeStrauss

www.ingramcontent.com/pod-product-compliance
Lightning Source LLC
Chambersburg PA
CBHW021959190626
46808CB00017B/2577